THE TRUTH ABOUT THE MARQUESS

WHISPERS OF THE TON (BOOK 3)

ROSE PEARSON

THE TRUTH ABOUT THE MARQUESS

*J*ane Casson, Countess of Harsham, closed her eyes, aware of the tension which ran through her.

"I must go back to London."

"Why must you?" Her sister, Emma Peterville, Lady Armitage, reached across to squeeze her hand. "You are happy here with us, are you not?"

Jane smiled softly, appreciating her sister's kindness.

"Of course I am. I am very happy indeed, but I cannot simply remain here for the rest of my days! You have your own husband and family and, fond though I am of my dear nephew and niece, I know that you would be best suited if I were not always present."

"How can you say that?" Tears sparked in Emma's eyes, and she withdrew her hand. "We have never once thought ill of your presence here. We have delighted in it, in fact!"

"I know that," Jane answered quickly, looking to soothe her sister's upset. "That is not what I meant. It is only to say that a family ought to be that – a family! I am very thankful for all that you have offered me, all that you have given me for these last two years, but the time has come where I must now permit you to return to your life and I must return to mine." She smiled gently, hoping that Emma would understand. "It is not that I am ungrateful, nor that I am eager to take my leave. It is only that I now must think of the future, and I know that I cannot stay here and rely on your kindness forever, even though I know it would be offered."

Emma nodded, dabbing at her eyes with her handkerchief which she had only just pulled from her sleeve.

"I understand what you mean. Though what will you do, Jane? What *can* you do?"

Jane let out a slow breath, aware of how her spirits quickly began to sink. She had been thinking of her future for some time and, as yet, had struggled to find any sort of clarity.

"I am not entirely certain. I think that I shall have to make my way to London for the Season."

"To marry again? After all that you endured with Lord Harsham?"

A slight shudder ran through Jane's frame, and she closed her eyes, the images of her late husband returning to her with such a fierceness that it made her tremble. The Earl of Harsham had been a cruel, uncompassionate gentleman who had thought nothing of Jane and her considerations. He had taken what he pleased, had done what he wished, and had berated her with fury and fierce anger every time that he perceived that she had done something that he considered to be wrong – which had been most of the time. Jane had once made the mistake of trying to speak to him about his lack of care for her, and that had brought about such a consequence that she had never dared to speak a single word to him on the matter again. Instead, she had become a quiet, obedient wife, who did not so much as look at her husband without his permission. Fear had been her constant companion, and when news had come of his death – killed by highwaymen who had come to steal what they could from his carriage – Jane had not felt one single ounce of grief. Instead, there had been relief and, with that, guilt. She ought not to be feeling glad over her husband's death, she had told herself, and thus, that had become a constant battle.

"You are thinking of him again." Emma's gentle voice broke through Jane's thoughts, and she started in surprise, blinking quickly as she looked back at her sister.

"I was, yes."

"You should not." Emma leaned forward in her chair just a little, her gaze searching Jane's face. "That man left bruises on you, bruises that you tried to hide from me, but that I saw anyway. He was not a good man. He was not a good husband! Do not let guilt pull you into any sort of darkness, my dear sister. I can see that it is threatening you, looming like a dark shadow in your eyes."

Jane closed her eyes so that she could shut out Emma's intense gaze. She knew that Emma was right, could practically feel the shadow that she spoke of looming over her but, all the same, she could not seem to free herself from it entirely.

"Our father should never have permitted Lord Harsham to take you as his bride," Emma muttered, just as Jane opened her eyes. "He knew the sort of gentleman Lord Harsham was, I am sure, while you and I did not."

"I cannot know for certain what Father had gleaned of Lord Harsham's character," Jane replied, feeling a slight defensiveness towards their late father. "Though he did gamble enough with him to know that he was foolish when it came to that, I am sure."

"Mayhap." Emma tilted her head. "And that must be of concern to you now, knowing how little you are to get once the present Lord Harsham does as he must." Emma's face screwed up in distaste. "Though the new Lord Harsham appears to be just as dreadful as his brother, given how little he cares for you! I could not believe my eyes when I read that letter from you, informing me that the newly titled Lord Harsham had told you to leave the house within a month. You, who had been wed to his brother! That is the most extraordinary thing."

Her chest tightened as Jane tried to push away the memories that her sister was bringing to mind. Whether she realized it or not, Emma was not being any great help to Jane, given what she was saying. It was everything that Jane was trying to put behind her, trying to forget about, and yet, Emma was pushing it to the fore again.

"Yes, my husband's brother was just as unkind as he was." Hoping that this would be enough to satisfy Emma, Jane spread out her hands. "But now, I must make the best of things, despite my lack of funds."

Emma's eyes narrowed just a fraction, taking Jane in.

"Does that mean that you intend to make your way to London in search of a new husband, then? You did not answer my question the first time."

Hesitating, Jane shook her head.

"I do not know, truth be told. I have been so wounded, that the idea of marrying again is quite terrifying. But yet, I recognize that I do require financial stability and, given the pittance that I am to receive from my late husband's will, it seems to me that the only way to do so is to marry. Though if there is any other way, then I shall find it!"

"Why do you not stay here?" Emma's voice had taken on a gentle pleading now, though Jane only smiled but shook her head. "You know that we would be glad to support you for the rest of your days, should you wish it! And my dear husband has already said he will deposit some money into your accounts so that you are not struggling in any way. Please, let us do this for you, Jane. After all you have suffered, ought you not now to let us care for you?"

The urge to give in to all that her sister offered was strong and, for a few moments, Jane fell silent, considering. Yes, she thought, it would be easy to remain at this estate, to help her sister care for the two children, but that would not necessarily be a good thing. Emma and her husband needed to run their estate and their home together, not with Jane's presence always with them, and she herself wanted something more, did she not? Even if it was not a husband, then that sense of freedom, that ability to do as she pleased without fear or consequence. Even with her limited funds, *that* was what she wanted.

"I do not think that I can, Emma." Speaking as gently as she could, Jane reached out to take her sister's hand, seeing the tears that immediately sparked in her eyes. "It is not because I do not wish it, not because I do not love you, nor that I am unhappy. It is because I think that it is for the best, for both you and your family, *and* me. Do you understand?"

Emma sniffed and dabbed at her nose but nodded.

"I do not want you to go."

"I know that. But I will return very often to visit. You are not so far away from London now, are you?"

Her sister's smile wobbled.

"No, I suppose we are not. Though," she continued, squeezing Jane's hand so tightly that it was a little painful, "will you not stay at our townhouse in London rather than find lodgings? That would be a help to you, would it not?"

Jane smiled.

"It would be, and I would be glad to accept."

Emma closed her eyes, her smile still present but sadness in it all the same.

"That is good. And I might have someone who could offer you something as regards your financial status, my dear Jane."

"Employment?" Astonished, Jane's eyebrows lifted high. "Who is it that you know who would employ a young lady, such as myself, as a governess?"

"Ah, but I did not say as a governess," came the reply, making Jane's brows fall into a frown. "You did not hear me say that."

"Then what would it be?" Jane grew a little irritated as her sister shrugged her shoulders. "Please, Emma, do not frustrate me so!"

Emma smiled and this time, it was without tears in her eyes.

"I cannot give you any details, not until I am sure that it might be a possibility, at the very least. But have no fear, it is something that you are going to be well able to do, I am sure. Something that will give you all the security you hope for."

Trying to push her irritation away, Jane turned her head away from her sister.

"Very well, I shall wait."

"Good." Emma beamed as Jane threw her a quick glance, either not in the least bit concerned, or barely even noticing Jane's frustration. "Now, shall we ring for tea?" Leaning back, she rubbed at her eyes, the other hand on her rounded stomach. "Though I am feeling rather fatigued."

"You go to rest," Jane suggested, getting to her feet. "I will ring the bell and serve the tea." Walking across the room, Jane was struck by a sudden sadness, a sadness which seemed to wash over her, She had lived here for two years now, and soon her time with her sister and family would come to an end. Here, it was comfortable and cozy, for she knew what was expected of her, knew her role, and that she was not being judged for anything she either said or did, unlike when she had been living with her late husband. To go to London, however, was entirely different - for there, many would speak about her, many would whisper about her, and she would have to do her best to quell the rumors – or try to ignore them as best she could. Could she do it? Or would she find it all too much to bear and, instead, rush back to the comfort and safety of the Armitage estate?

CHAPTER ONE

"I do not understand." Scowling, Oliver Marston, Marquess of Edenbridge, rubbed one hand over his face and then shook his head. "I have done all that I can to convince Lady Anna that I am sincere and yet, she continued to flirt with every gentleman present!"

"But you cannot blame yourself for that," came the reply, a heavy hand settling on Oliver's shoulder. "You know as well as I do that there are many young ladies here in London who will care nothing for any of the gentlemen that they might offer some attention to!"

Oliver scowled.

"I do not much like that."

His friend, the Earl of Dunstable, grinned broadly.

"I am sure that you do not, but that is the way of things. The young women here are all seeking an excellent match, in way of both title and fortune."

"Both of which I have."

"Ah, but what of your fortune?" Lord Dunstable winced as Oliver threw him a sharp look. "You have been in

London ever since you were a young lad out of Eton. The *ton* knows of your father and his lack of wealth when it came to the end of his days here on earth. Now, however, they also know that *you* have been bearing the burden of repairing that situation and that your fortune does not match the fortunes of others of your standing." Oliver's shoulders dropped as Lord Dunstable continued, a sudden heaviness planting itself upon his shoulders. "Yes, my friend, they will offer you smiles and bright eyes, but they may not offer you anything more than that. Not until they can be sure that you are their best choice!"

Scowling, Oliver looked away, heat on his face.

"I am aware that I do not have the very best of fortunes, all thanks to my father and his foolish investments, but I have worked hard to improve it." Oliver rubbed one hand over his face. "Nor do I know if society believes me in that regard either, for no matter what I say, the words seem to be lost on the wind. I see the suspicion in their glances and hear the whispers being passed between them. I find it all quite exhausting, truth be told."

"Making your fortune again has been tiring, I am sure, but does it still continue to be such a weight upon you?"

Oliver shook his head.

"No, it is not that which tires me, it is being amongst these young ladies!" He waved one hand vaguely across the ballroom. "It is quite ridiculous, is it not? I have young ladies *themselves* to impress at the first, and that is difficult in itself, despite my title and good standing! Thereafter, I have mothers or fathers to consider me and even then, it seems I might not find approval! What am I to do then?"

Lord Dunstable chuckled ruefully.

"I do not know. Mayhap you might seek an arrangement?"

"A match of convenience, you mean." Oliver grimaced, looking out across the ballroom and finding his whole being removing itself from that idea. "No, I do not think so."

"But you want to marry!" his friend exclaimed, throwing up his hands. "Many a happy match has been made in such a way, why would you turn from that?"

"Because many an *unhappy* marriage has such a match made," Oliver answered, shuddering slightly. "I think of my own parents. My dear father and mother, though they were excellent parents and very dutiful towards each other, had no happiness. Indeed, I believe that my mother was at her happiest when my father was away from home! The times that he had to go abroad for business made her almost gleeful!"

Lord Dunstable's mouth tugged to one side as he considered. There was quietness from him for a few minutes, only for him to then shrug.

"You cannot say that all are like that, however. There must be some matches which are very happy indeed! You might be fortunate and have such a match."

"Or I might be unfortunate and have a match that brings me nothing but disappointment and upset," Oliver answered, making Lord Dunstable's expression pull into a scowl. "I hardly think that I should risk such a thing, do you?"

Lord Dunstable hesitated, then sighed.

"I do not have any further advice for you. I confess that I am uncertain as to what it is that has driven you to this desire to marry and thus, though I have said what I can to support it, there is nothing more for me to add."

Accepting this, Oliver looked around the ballroom again and then closed his eyes briefly, feeling a sense of frustration building within him.

"It is my responsibility to find a wife," he said, half to himself and half to his friend. "I must find a suitable match with a lady who is going to be kind, considerate, and dutiful. However, that does not mean that a match of convenience will bring me all of that. Instead, I fear it might bring me the opposite!"

"And so you are determined to find a match of love?"

Oliver considered this.

"Not necessarily of love, but of genuine care, and even a little affection, yes." Sighing, he let his jaw tighten for a moment, pushing away some of his irritation by doing so. "It appears that such a thing is going to be very hard to find, however. I do not think that it will be as easy as I had first thought, given the way that I was just now rejected by Lady Anna."

"You shall simply have to keep trying, that is all." Lord Dunstable chuckled as Oliver scowled. "Or you can give up the notion and become a scoundrel, if you wish it?"

That made Oliver laugh, aware that his friend was jesting.

"I hardly think that such a thing would be agreeable to anyone, for I would be even less likely to find someone willing to marry me should I do so! Besides which, there are far too many rogues in London already, are there not?"

"There are." This made the laughter fall from Lord Dunstable's expression. "Far too many." Heaving a sigh, he rolled his eyes. "One might think that the young ladies of London would then be drawn to gentlemen who were *not* such a way inclined, but it seems that there are many where that is not the case!"

It feels as though I may as well give up before I have even begun! Oliver ran one hand over his face, aware of a sudden heaviness in his limbs. He had come to London, hopeful and determined, had found himself drawn to one young lady and had pursued her carefully. Lady Anna had taken his attentions with evident gladness, smiling and blushing and expressing all manner of interest towards him – only for her to state that no, she would not accept his courtship... not as yet, anyway. Oliver had not understood, had thought that it might mean that she wanted him to fight all the more for her attention, only to then see her flirting and laughing with various other gentlemen at the ball this evening. Clearly, she was not as impressed with him as a potential suitor as he had thought, though she had given the impression that he was the only one she had any sort of interest in.

"You will succeed in time, I am sure." Lord Dunstable smiled briefly, but Oliver only shook his head. "Do not let Lady Anna dissuade you from trying to find the right young lady to marry."

"Mayhap," Oliver murmured, not in the least bit convinced. "As much as I do not want to have an arranged marriage, it may be that I will have to. If I get to the end of the Season without making any sort of progress, then I will have to consider it."

~

"LADY JANICE."

Oliver inclined his head, then smiled as warmly as he could. Lady Janice was a young lady who was in her second Season and Oliver had been introduced to her the previous year. He thought her pretty, she seemed rather kind, and Oliver did find himself a *little* drawn to her.

"How very kind of you to call, Lord Edenbridge." Lady Janice smiled, as she curtsied, along with her mother, Lady Kirkton. "Might I ask if you would like some tea?"

"I should." Oliver sat down and smiled, finding himself a little pleased with how welcoming the lady was being to him. "Thank you." He watched as Lady Janice poured the tea for him, appreciating all the more the gentle smile that the lady offered him as she set the tea down in front of him. "I thank you. Might I ask if you are enjoying the Season, Lady Janice?"

She nodded.

"I am indeed." Pouring more tea, she offered a cup to her mother and then sat down herself, smiling still. "I think that there is a good deal still to come as well, which I am very excited about!"

"Tell me, do you enjoy the balls or the soirees better?" Oliver asked, only for there to come a knock at the door.

"Oh, do excuse me," Lady Kirkton said, before calling to the butler to come in.

Oliver kept his smile fixed, looking across at Lady Janice and considering just how pretty she was. There was a light-ness in her eyes, the gentlest of smiles on her face, and a hint of color in her cheeks. Surely this was someone that he might consider! And who, he hoped, might consider him!

"Lord Brackston!"

Oliver frowned as he watched another gentleman walk into the room. Lady Janice's eyes lit up in a way that they had not done when he had come into the room and, instantly, Oliver felt all of his hopes begin to fade. Closing his eyes, Oliver let out a long, slow breath and then shook his head to himself.

"Lord Brackston, you are acquainted with Lord Eden-bridge, I hope?"

Oliver rose to his feet quickly, smiling, though he felt like doing the opposite.

"Yes, we are. How do you do?"

He shook the gentleman's hand and then sat down again, silently berating himself for his lack of belief. Yes, Lady Janice seemed to be pleased with the arrival of Lord Brackston, but that did not mean that *he* did not have a chance with her, did it? After all, they were not all that well acquainted and there was no reason why he could not pursue her! Clearly, Lord Brackston had not done so as yet, otherwise he would have heard of their courtship! Feeling a little more encouraged, Oliver settled back in his seat, smiling with ease now.

"Might I pour you some tea, Lord Brackston?" Lady Janice asked, as the gentleman she spoke to also sank into his seat. "I have only just now poured a cup for Lord Eden-bridge, and it will be hot enough still, I am sure."

"Though we can send for a fresh pot if you so require it," her mother added quickly, sounding a little flustered. "Whatever you require, Lord Brackston."

The gentleman waved one hand.

"Tea, as it is, will be more than acceptable, I assure you. Though," he continued, as Oliver reached for his own cup, "I must say that I had come to speak with you, Lady Janice, in the hope of more than a simple cup of tea."

Silence fell for a few moments, though Oliver's stomach then began to tighten, a warning beginning to ring through his mind. Somehow, he knew what was coming.

"Might I beg of you to consider accepting an offer of my courtship?" Lord Brackston sounded a little breathless as Lady Janice froze in place, the teapot in her hand wobbling just a little. "You know that I think you quite wonderful and that I should very much like to court you, my dear."

Oliver closed his eyes, hearing the way Lady Janice's teapot now clattered onto the table. There was a sudden exclamation from her mother and Oliver, opening his eyes, rose to his feet, bowed, and left the room.

No one seemed to notice, for not a word was spoken to him. Instead, all he heard was Lady Janice's excited voice accepting Lord Brackston's request and the expression of delight that soon followed from Brackston. Wincing, he stepped out into the hallway and then after collecting his hat and cane from the butler, he hurried out of the front door and back towards his carriage, feeling a flush of embarrassment fill him.

He had not known that there had been any real interest between Lady Janice and Lord Brackston. Instead, all he had seen was a young lady who pleased him and, thereafter, had considered pursuing her instead of Lady Anna! If he had been a little more considered, a little more careful, then he might never have made such a mistake, nor felt such disappointment.

Sighing, he climbed into the carriage and, closing his eyes, sank back against the squabs.

It feels as though I am to have no success! That I shall fail in everything I try.

The carriage began to move, and Oliver tried to push away his embarrassment, though it still clung to him. He had to pray that neither Lady Janice nor Lord Brackston would tell anyone else in the *ton* that he had been present during their conversation, for no doubt someone would ask why he had been there – and he would have no choice but to tell them!

For the first time, the notion of an arranged marriage seemed a little pleasant to his mind, though he tried to steady himself and reconsider. He had always wanted affection and care in whatever future he had with a lady of the *ton* and he could not, *would* not give up now.

No matter how difficult it seemed.

CHAPTER TWO

"Jane?"

"Yes?" Smiling, Jane set her basket full of flowers on her arm and came towards her sister. "My goodness, you look quite wonderful, Emma!"

Her sister blushed and looked down at her new gown.

"I thank you. I do not often purchase new gowns when we are not going to London, but I thought that I would like to now. Do you think that he will like it?"

Jane smiled softly.

"I think that your husband will think you look quite beautiful," she said, seeing how her sister's blush grew. "I have seen how much he cares for you, my dear. I think that you will delight him all the more in this gown!"

Emma smoothed out an invisible crease, her lips curving gently.

"I thank you, Jane. I do wish that you would join us this evening."

"I was not included in the invitation," Jane reminded her, quietly. "That is not to say that I am in the least bit upset by it or that I think that Lord and Lady Franks ought to have done so, but to remind you that my presence is not expected."

"Oh, but there was that note which came thereafter, do you not remember?" Sounding eager, Emma put a hand on Jane's arm. "They wished you to know that you would be welcome to join them also, though they knew that your preparations for London were of great importance."

Nodding, Jane smiled at her sister but then gestured to the flowers.

"I am quite contented doing this, I assure you. Collecting spring flowers and then putting them into arrangements will offer me a great deal of pleasure, I assure you. I do not need to go to any soiree. Besides which," she continued, a little softer now, "I *am* soon to go to London. It is not as though I shall be present here any longer."

"But that does not mean–"

"Please, Emma, do not worry!" Taking her sister's hand, she pressed it gently. "You need not be upset. I am more than contented, I assure you. Besides, who will look after your two children this evening if I do not stay?"

"The maids? The governess? The nursemaid?" Emma rolled her eyes, though she did smile when Jane laughed quietly. "You know that I am concerned for you, my dear sister."

"You need not be. Besides, you will not be able to see all that I do once I am in London!"

Her sister's smile grew a little sad.

"I will miss you."

"As I will you."

Emma sniffed, took in a deep breath and then lifted her chin, looking at Jane straight in the eye.

"I must tell you that I have made some arrangements for you, once you are in London."

Jane's smile shattered.

"Arrangements?"

With a nod, Jane gestured to the bench a short distance away and together, the two sisters walked to it and sat down together. A little nervous, Jane looked at her sister steadily, her stomach lurching as Emma smiled. She caught the slight glint in Emma's eye, wondering just what it was that her sister had planned. She hoped that it was not some new scheme to keep her here rather than permitting her to go to London!

"I know that you have spoken of finding yourself financial security," Emma began, as Jane set her basket of flowers to one side. "I also know that you believe you will have to marry to find such a thing."

"It is the only thing that a young lady can do, is it not?" Jane replied, a slight frown brushing across her forehead. "I do not have the opportunity to pursue else, anything other than perhaps becoming a governess, which is not something I wish to do. The thought of becoming a spinster and fearing for my future every day of my life, even whilst caring for someone else's children, is not a pleasing one, though you know very well that I care deeply for *your* children."

Emma laughed softly and put her hand on Jane's for a moment.

"Of course I do. They dote upon you! Though I quite understand what it is you mean when you speak of being fearful of your future – and it is *that* fear that I wish to address."

"What do you mean?"

Emma took a deep breath and then set her shoulders.

"My husband and I are to give you the townhouse."

It felt as though something had wrapped around Jane's

chest, constricting her breathing. She stared at her sister, a slight hissing in her ears as Emma searched her face in return, clearly looking for Jane's response.

"You... you are *giving* me the townhouse?"

"Yes." Emma beamed though Jane could feel nothing but astonishment. "We want you never to be concerned about where you shall live and, truth be told, my husband has been seeking a new townhouse in London. He does not much like the present townhouse, stating that it is too small for our requirements, though I disagree with him! However, he has suggested – and it was *he* who suggested it – that we give you the townhouse as your permanent abode and, therefore, you will have no concerns over where you shall live."

"I... I do not know what to say." Jane put one hand to her throat, rubbing there gently in an attempt to encourage herself to breathe a little more easily. "I do not think that you need to do such a thing for me, Emma, though I am overwhelmed with gratitude. You must tell Lord Armitage the same."

Emma shook her head.

"It is not because I *need* to, but because I want to, Jane. I have found what you have not; a kind, compassionate, considerate gentleman for a husband and, though I want you to find the very same thing, I am aware – as is Armitage – that there is an uncertainty within you when it comes to even considering that possibility. Therefore, we wanted to do what we could to support you, seeing your selflessness when you consider returning to London to return the estate to our family entirely. Though I still do not think there is a need for you to do so."

Jane laughed, though it came out as a broken sound, shaking her head.

"Even if I could simply reside there until such a time as my circumstances change, then I would be content with that. You do not need to make it my property."

Her sister shrugged.

"I shall leave that up to Armitage and his solicitors. But you will accept?"

A part of Jane wanted to thank her sister, but refuse to accept it, as a sense of determination to live alone and care for herself as best she could rose to the fore. But after a moment, she smiled, pressed her sister's hand, and nodded. There was no need for pride here, not at this moment.

"Thank you, I shall." Taking in a deep breath, she let it out slowly, relief beginning to fill her. "I will be able to have a good deal more security now, though I shall still have to be careful with my finances." Seeing the way that Emma opened her mouth, Jane shook her head quickly. "No, Emma, you and Armitage have done enough. I shall not take more from you."

Her sister chuckled.

"I told my dear husband that you would say that! But be assured, I have no intention of offering you coin, for I knew that you would not accept. However, I have found you some employment."

Another ripple of shock ran through Jane's frame.

"Employment?"

Emma nodded, her face wreathed with smiles though Jane herself did not smile, wondering what it was that Emma had come up with.

"It is an excellent position, one which will support you with a little more coin but, at the same time, private enough that the *ton* will not know of it!"

All the more confused, Jane frowned heavily.

"I do not understand."

"It is an anonymous position!" Emma exclaimed, as though this explained everything. "There will be letters sent to you seeking advice on various situations and all you have to do is reply!"

Rubbing one hand lightly over her forehead, Jane took a few moments of quiet to calm her confusion and growing frustration.

"Emma, you are not making any sense to me. Please, explain what you mean. What employment is this?"

Her sister bit her lip, then looked away.

"My apologies. I am, mayhap, being a little overexcited." The smile quickly returned, however, her eyes bright. "There is a newspaper in London, do you recall it? 'The London Chronicle'?"

Jane nodded slowly, still struggling to understand what her sister was talking about.

"Yes, I know the paper. I do not often read it."

"It has become rather popular, I believe, and I am well acquainted with the lady who, at the first, began it all. Knowing your dilemma and how well the paper served *her*, I wrote to ask if there was any way she might be able to consider supporting you in the same way. She replied to me and told me that there was a requirement for someone to take up a position with The London Chronicle."

Something that felt like excitement caught Jane's heart, though she quietened it quickly, still not fully under-standing what it was that Emma had found for her.

"I would be writing for a paper?"

"For 'The London Chronicle', yes." Emma spoke a little more slowly now, as though she were explaining something to a small child. "They have started a section within the newspaper where those in the *ton* can write anonymously to the editor, seeking advice on some situation or the next. It has proven very popular indeed and now, they seek someone to employ to respond to those letters regularly. I have looked into the pay offered and I think it would suit you very well!"

Jane considered this, tilting her head just a little.

"I am not certain that I would always know what to say."

"I think that you would – and if you did not, then I am sure that there would be others you could speak to, *before* you responded publicly," came the reply, Emma's enthusiasm undampened by Jane's hesitation. "Think of it, Jane! It means that you would be able to reside in London, be a part of society, enjoy the company of the *ton* but have no requirement to marry – while, at the same time, making certain that your finances were well supported with this little employment! It would not take up a good deal of your time, I am sure, and you would also be able to remain entirely anonymous if you wished."

"So my reputation would not be spoken of," Jane murmured, "though I do not think that there can be any great criticism of someone who writes for a newspaper!" Her sister smiled but said nothing, her eyes still filled with a brightness that Jane could not help but respond to. "You are very kind to have done so much for me, Emma," she said, leaning forward so that she could embrace her sister. "To have you so considered and concerned has touched my heart."

"But of course." Leaning back, Emma's smile remained, though Jane caught the flicker of tears in her eyes. "I want to see you happy again, Jane. I thought at first that it might be in finding another gentleman to marry, one who might leave you feeling happy and contented, but I see now that such a thing is not the *only* way for you to be so."

Jane nodded, her throat tight again though, this time, it came from tears of gratitude over her sister's thoughtfulness.

"Might I ask if you will consider it?" Emma asked, quietly. "Will you think of it for a time, at the very least?"

Pressing her lips together, Jane lifted her chin and, despite the quailing of her heart, spread out her hands.

"I do not need to think about it. It is, as you have said, a way to support myself but without the need for matrimony. So yes, Emma, I shall accept the employment and write for 'The London Chronicle'."

CHAPTER THREE

"I hear that Lady Janice is now courting."

Oliver scowled at his friend, though Lord Dunstable only grinned.

"Yes, I am well aware of that."

"Was that not someone that you were thinking to call upon?"

A slight flush came over Oliver's face.

"Yes, I did. I mean, yes, I was going to."

Lord Dunstable's eyebrows rose.

"You called on her?"

Oliver winced, wishing that he had not misspoken in such an obvious way.

"Yes, I did. In fact, I did call upon her, at the very time that Lord Brackston did also." Seeing the way that his friend's lips quirked, Oliver let out a groan, knowing that he would be unable to escape his friend's inquisitiveness. "Lord Brackston came into the room, greeted the ladies, and thereafter, practically fell upon his knees and begged Lady Janice to allow him to court her! Just as I was thinking that there was nothing about Lady Janice that I did not like, thinking to myself that I might very easily begin to pursue her, only for Lord Brackston to interrupt my plans!"

"How very rude of him," Lord Dunstable chuckled, his mouth broad in a smile. "Though that is not necessarily a bad thing, is it? It means that you had no need to pursue her, only to then realize that Lord Brackston was interested in her also. That has saved you a great deal of time and effort, I think."

"I suppose so." Oliver let out another sigh, reaching to take a drink from a passing footman's tray. "It does make me feel that there is very little hope for me, I must confess. First, I had Lady Anna's rejection and now, I have been pushed away before I even had the chance to draw close to Lady Janice!"

"But do not give up yet," Lord Dunstable said, quickly. "I will help you, I think."

Oliver's eyebrows lifted.

"You want to help me find a bride?"

"If it stops your complaining and whining, then I think that I would be more than willing to do anything you asked!" came the reply, though Lord Dunstable grinned with it, making Oliver roll his eyes, though he could not help but smile also. "Yes, I think I shall. And mayhap I shall find myself a bride at the very same time!"

This made Oliver laugh, knowing that his friend was a dedicated bachelor and had no intention whatsoever of becoming attached to any young lady.

"Now I know that you are jesting."

"I certainly am not!" Lord Dunstable replied, only to chuckle as he shrugged his shoulders. "Very well, I say that I *may* find myself a bride but the chances of doing such a thing are very faint indeed. It would have to be a very special young lady, and a very *intriguing* young lady, to capture my attention, I am sure! But all the same, I would be glad to be of aid to you, seeing that you are so very fervent – both in what you seek and in what you hope for!"

"Well, I would be grateful for it, I am sure." Looking out across the ballroom, Oliver let out a long, heavy sigh and shook his head. "I seem to be failing before I have even begun!"

A more serious look came over Lord Dunstable's expression as he surveyed the room.

"The first thing we must do is to have your dance card entirely filled. After all, you are a Marquess – albeit one with a slightly smaller fortune compared to others – but that should not be too difficult a thing to overcome! There will be many a young lady who will not be too concerned about that, I am sure, especially if you make it plain that you are doing all you can to improve it of late! I will make sure that I speak of that to as many of the *ton* as I can, and that will improve your standing all the more."

Oliver nodded, rubbing one hand over his chin. That was his only flaw, he was sure. To have a slightly diminished fortune did mean that the *ton* looked at him with a little more concern, and did not instantly consider him to be as eligible as others.

"That will help."

"Well? What are you waiting for?" Lord Dunstable threw one hand out as though to sweep Oliver towards the crowd before him. "Take yourself to the *ton* and have as many young ladies on your dance card as you can!"

"I – I thought you would help me?" Confused, Oliver did not take another step. "I will do what I have always done, dancing with various young ladies – and then what shall I do?"

"Ah-ha!" Lord Dunstable tapped the side of his nose.

"Then, you can return to my company, and I will look at your dance card and inform you of which young lady you might then consider pursuing. You know that I am well-informed about society and those within it, so I would hope that I can help you there."

A slight lift of Oliver's heart made the edges of his lips curve up. Finally, he felt a little hope.

"Yes, I suppose that you shall," he agreed, for Lord Dunstable was a very popular gentleman within London, with his title, excellent character, substantial fortune, and his easy smiles – as well as the fact that he had not yet taken a bride! "That is kind of you to be willing to assist me, my friend."

"Of course."

Lord Dunstable lifted one eyebrow and, with a nod, Oliver made his way out into the crowd.

His eyes scanned the room, taking in one face after another. Yes, he had been in London for many a Season already and was known to the *ton,* but that meant they *also* knew about his past financial struggles. He could only hope that Lord Dunstable's offer of help would prove to be beneficial. Letting his gaze alight on one small group of young ladies, Oliver's heart lifted just a little. There were, he recognized, three that he was already acquainted with and two that he was not – and what better way to fill his dance card than by greeting them *all* without hesitation?

"Lady Norah, Lady Jemima, Miss Dutton." Oliver bowed his head low, keeping his smile pinned as he then looked up and smiled. "How very good to see you all here this evening."

Lady Norah and Lady Jemima shared a glance, and both curtsied. Miss Dutton, however, smiled warmly and dropped into a quick curtsey, barely taking her eyes from his.

"We are enjoying the evening here, Lord Edenbridge," Miss Dutton told him, her green eyes warm. "I am glad to see you again. I think it was last Season when we last spoke!"

"It may well have been." A little surprised by the lady's enthusiasm, Oliver turned to the ladies he did not know, keeping his smile fixed. "Might you introduce me to your acquaintances?"

"But of course!" Miss Dutton was more than enthusiastic, quickly introducing him to Miss Quillon and Lady Victoria, who both were warm in their greeting, though not as effervescent as Miss Dutton, who appeared to be more than delighted in all that Oliver said and did. That in itself was rather unusual, for they were not particularly well acquainted.

I have only just been complaining to Lord Dunstable about the lack of genuine interest from various young ladies. Am I really going to be suspicious of a young lady merely because she appears to be warming to my company?

Telling himself that he was being ridiculous, Oliver looked around the group, his gaze lingering on Miss Dutton. She had fair hair and pale blue eyes with a kind smile and that, he was sure, spoke of a good character.

"I do hope that some of you will dance this evening? As yet, I have no one to stand up with and I should very much like to dance as many dances as possible!"

Before any other young lady could do so, Miss Dutton practically flung her dance card at him, her eyes wide with evident excitement.

"I should be delighted!"

Oliver took it from her, then quickly wrote his name in the very first dance he could find available.

"Here, Miss Dutton. I do hope that the cotillion will suffice?"

"Oh, but of course!"

She took it with eager fingers, but Oliver was already looking around at the others, doing his best not to focus entirely on what Miss Dutton was offering by way of her keenness for his company. He reminded himself that he had already failed in his pursuit by focusing on only one lady. He had to do as Lord Dunstable had suggested and make sure that he danced with as many young ladies as possible. Mayhap then he might have a greater chance of success when the time came to move forward with only one.

"I should be glad to dance with you, Lord Edenbridge," Miss Quillon said, handing him her dance card. "Thank you for your kindness."

Oliver took it from her, confidence beginning to fill him as he wrote his name down for the polka. Lady Jemima and Lady Norah each folded their arms, evidently making it clear that they were not interested in dancing with him. That took some of Oliver's confidence away, though he did his best to appear outwardly contented.

"I thank you," he murmured, handing the card back to Miss Quillon, just as Lady Victoria slipped her dance card from her wrist. "Lady Victoria, I–"

"Might I ask, Lord Edenbridge, whether you have still a great difficulty with your father's poor investments?"

Oliver blinked, suddenly frozen in place, his hand only half reaching out towards Lady Victoria.

"I beg your pardon?"

Lady Jemima lifted her chin, her gaze a little icy.

"Everyone in London knows that you did not inherit a

fortune and that your estate is in need of some repair. Might I ask if those difficulties have become any heavier upon your shoulders? I must sympathize with you, I am sure, for it is not your fault that you have inherited such troubles."

Out of the corner of his eye, Oliver caught Lady Victoria beginning to retract her hand, her dance card still clasped in it. Quickly, he reached out and took it from her, suddenly filled with an intense dislike for Lady Jemima and her bold words.

"I do not know what you have heard, Lady Jemima, but there are some untruths, some whispers being spoken of me of late which are most unfortunate indeed," he said, firmly, dropping his gaze to Lady Victoria's dance card. "I would not like anyone to have the wrong impression about my standing, financially or otherwise."

"Hmph." Lady Jemima sniffed, sharing a look with Lady Norah. "Then you mean to say that you have returned your fortune to the great heights it must once have been?"

Oliver scowled but quickly changed his expression as best he could, bending his head to write his name on Lady Victoria's dance card. He was now rather suspicious that she would be notably absent when the time came for them to dance, given her obvious reluctance.

"I am grateful for your sympathy, Lady Jemima," he said, lifting his head and handing the card back to Lady Victoria with what he hoped was a smile on his lips. Given the sheer amount of tension running through him, he could not say that he had succeeded in a natural smile. "I have worked hard to improve my situation, and I am glad to say that there has been a considerable amount of... improvement." Aware that he had used the same word twice in the same sentence, and irritated with himself that he had not been able to speak more effectively, he spread out his hands. "I do hope that answers your question."

"Mmm." Lady Norah spoke this time, her eyebrows lifting gently. "Do you mean to say that, though there has been *some* increase, there has been nothing substantial? Does your manor house require some improvements still?"

Heat built in his chest as Oliver gazed back into Lady Norah's eyes, hoping that his steady gaze would deter her from her question but instead, all that happened was that she arched an eyebrow, waiting for his response – and Oliver had no choice but to give it.

"I think, Lady Norah, that I would not be here in London and in the midst of society, if I did not think myself to be suitably situated, both in terms of fortune and in my estate. Truth be told, I find it rather disappointing to be asked so many questions as though I must prove myself in such a way rather than having people consider my character and my heart!" Seeing how Lady Norah looked away, Oliver continued, his chest filling with air as he puffed it out, hoping that she would feel a little embarrassed to have spoken so, given his response. "It is not the sort of thing which I have asked any of you now, is it?"

"That is because we have no great fortune, Lord Edenbridge," Lady Norah replied quickly, her gaze swinging back towards him. "All that we have belongs to our fathers."

"And I have not asked you questions about them, have I?" Oliver responded, aware that his voice was growing a little louder now, his hands curling tight as he tried to keep hold of himself. Embarrassment was what drove him, mortification over what had been asked, and still, he continued. "I have not stood here and enquired as to what each of your dowries shall be, nor whether or not your fathers have enough funds to keep them respectable! All I have asked is to dance, Lady Norah, and if you wish to refuse, then so be it. I would only ask that you be a trifle more considerate in practically berating me over my lack of fortune – a situation which was not of my making and which I have been burdened with repairing, ever since I stepped into the title." He stopped then, breathing hard as he looked around the small group. Some of the ladies were staring at him with wide eyes, others were looking down at the floor whilst others – most notably, Lady Norah and Lady Jemima – had slight lifts to the edges of their lips, in what Oliver took to be mocking smiles. He closed his eyes briefly, clearing his throat as he did so. "Do excuse me. I look forward to dancing with *some* of you later this evening."

"I am still looking forward to it, Lord Edenbridge!"

Oliver managed only a small nod in the direction of Miss Dutton as he turned away, his face flaming. Thus far, he had managed to not only embarrass himself in front of that small group of ladies but also managed to damage his own reputation by speaking as he had done. Yes, he had defended himself, but in doing so, he had spoken much too harshly and much too bluntly, no doubt making some of the young ladies think rather poorly of him. He dropped his head, groaning inwardly, rubbing one hand over his eyes. He had answered as honestly as he could, as regarded his fortune, but he had seen in their eyes that it was not the answer they had wanted. It seemed that, to improve his reputation and his standing, he had to have restored his fortune to a size even greater than it had been before, had to have made improvements to every part of his estate, rather than just the parts which needed repair... and he could not do that!

"Well?"

Oliver looked up to see Lord Dunstable coming to join him, a look of expectation on his face.

"I – I do not want to speak about what just happened."

"No?" Lord Dunstable's eyes widened. "Whyever not?"

"Because I have made a fool of myself," Oliver replied, his heart sinking low. "And even though I have a few dances now filled, I am quite sure that none of them will wish to dance with me again." His spirits sank even lower, and he shook his head, aware of the many questions which Lord Dunstable wished to ask him, but having no desire to answer even one of them. "I think that I shall find a drink and then a quiet corner of the room," he continued, before his friend could say anything. "It seems, I fear, that no matter what I try, I am going to be doomed to failure."

"I am sure that is not so," his friend replied quickly, but Oliver only turned away and walked directly to the back of the ballroom, eager to be alone.

His shoulders rounded and his head dropped as he found the shadows of the room welcoming him, rushing into them as though he rushed into the arms of a lady he loved.

Except all that met him was silence.

CHAPTER FOUR

Swallowing her fears, Jane lifted her gaze and began to walk through London's Hyde Park, leaving her carriage behind her. Her brother-in-law had been very generous indeed – though Jane had protested, of course - but he had been most insistent. She now not only had a townhouse of her own, but also a carriage and horses, as well as a whole host of servants to care for her and the house. There had been a great many tears upon her departure, tears from Jane herself, as well as from her sister and family, but it still had not deterred her. She was now quite determined to make her way in London and to see what the future might hold for her, though now with the assurance of income and employment, Jane certainly felt far more at ease. There was no longer the fear of being left alone, without funds and hope, no longer the concern that she would have to become a governess and scrape for as much money as she could so that she could live out her final days in vague comfort. No, there now came a sense of freedom, of hope and anticipation, and Jane was grateful for that.

Though coming back to London has been a good deal more overwhelming than I had ever anticipated.

Keeping her head held high and a light smile on her face, Jane continued to wander through the Park, silently wondering if anyone would greet her. Mayhap society had forgotten about her, for it had been two years since she had last been among them – and it had only been her second Season when she had been wed to Lord Harsham. It felt rather strange to be walking alone, without a chaperone or friend beside her. When she had last been in London, the requirement had been that she would always be with someone, would always be present beside either her father or her sister but, now, given that she was a widow, it was entirely acceptable for her to walk on her own.

"Jane?" Hearing her name, Jane continued walking, though she slowed her steps, uncertain as to whether she had heard correctly. It was most unusual for anyone to be called by their Christian name, especially when they were out in public! "Jane, is that you?"

Stopping, Jane turned around, only for her eyes to flare wide as her breath caught in her chest.

"Louisa?"

The next moment, she was enveloped in a tight embrace, her dearest friend in all the world holding her tight. Tears came into Jane's eyes as she stepped back, grasping Louisa's hands, barely able to make out a word her friend was saying, despite the torrent that was pouring from her lips.

"I am sorry," she found herself saying, over and over. "I am so sorry, Louisa."

"Sorry?" Her friend squeezed her hands, tears now on her cheeks. "What are you apologizing for?"

"I did not write to you." Jane closed her eyes, recalling how her husband had torn up her letters in front of her eyes, refusing to let her send even the smallest greeting to anyone. "I tried but–"

"I understand. Please, you need not be upset. I understand the difficulties you faced."

Confused as to how her friend could know such a thing, Jane frowned.

"I do not... oh. Emma."

Her friend nodded.

"Yes, Emma told me all. When I did not hear from you, I wrote to her directly, begging to know if all was well. She told me that your marriage to Lord Harsham was not a happy one, that you found yourself in a great deal of difficulty, and that she had not received a letter from you in some time, despite writing very often." A small, sad smile touched her friend's lips. "I understood it then to be that Lord Harsham must have been preventing your letters."

"That and a good deal more," Jane answered, heavily. "I am so very glad to see you again, Louisa. And I am all the more relieved that you are not angry and upset with me! I know that I could have written to you once I returned to my sister's estate, but the truth is, I was not certain what you would say or do, should I have done so. I felt so much guilt and shame and... in truth, all manner of emotions, I often felt my heart torn by confusion and doubt. How glad I am that you have not turned aside from me."

"I could never do so," her friend promised. "How glad I am to see you in London! Are you come for the Season?"

Jane nodded, tilting her head.

"Just so that I might be back in society again and, I suppose, to think about my future and what I must do. Though you are here again for a match, I suppose?"

"Not I!" A warm smile spread across the lady's face. "I was a truly dreadful daughter and eloped with Lord Guilford last Season!"

Jane's mouth fell open in astonishment as Lady Guilford giggled, her cheeks pinking.

"You... you eloped?"

"I had no choice! My father was insistent that I consider Lord Soutar, a gentleman from the very farthest town in Scotland, and I had no interest in him whatsoever! Particularly after there was a scandal with a young lady by the name of Miss Dutton, though Lord Soutar insists it was *she* who encouraged him, rather than the other way around." Her smile grew. "I wanted to be in the arms of Lord Guilford and, thus, since my father would have refused his request to court me, we chose to drive to Scotland and marry there." She shrugged. "He does not have as high a title as Lord Soutar, for he is a Viscount whereas Lord Soutar an Earl, but I do not care for such things. I am very happy indeed and I am certain I always shall be, now that I am wed to the gentleman I love."

"Goodness." Jane put one hand to her stomach, her breath hitching. "That is astonishing, though I am glad to hear of your happiness!"

Her friend smiled and the softness in her eyes made Jane's lips curve also. It was clear that Louisa was very happy indeed, and Jane was truly delighted to see it.

"Are you now in London simply to enjoy the Season?"

"Yes, that is so." Taking Jane's arm, Louisa turned and the two began to walk together. "Though how wonderful it shall be, now that *you* are here!"

"I confess that I am very glad to see you. I was filled with anxiety about walking through the park alone, hopeful that someone – anyone – would remember me! I did not think that to have no one to speak with would make for a very pleasant afternoon."

Louisa smiled gently.

"My dear friend, you are altered, though not so much that *I* would not recognize you. I must say, I am glad that you are free of Lord Harsham." She winced as she spoke, sending a sidelong glance toward Jane. "I do not mean to say that I am glad that he has passed away, that is not what I mean in the least."

"I understand what you mean, for I confess that I feel it myself." Jane let out a slow breath, then shook her head. "I should tell you that the new Lord Harsham had me removed from the estate just as soon as he was able, which is why I sought refuge with my sister and her husband. My late husband did not leave me any sort of income either, for I was barely mentioned in the will!"

"Goodness! Then he was even more of a cruel sort than I thought him!"

Jane nodded, her gaze now on the path before them, rather than looking at her friend.

"I have enough to pay for my food, and mayhap a maid and one footman but nothing more – and that would be difficult enough! I did not have a place to live aside from my sister's estate and thus, I came to London with the initial intention of finding a husband, though I confess I was loath to do so."

"I quite understand."

Jane took in another breath, a little surprised at just how overwhelmed she was in telling Lousia all of this.

"I told my sister all of this and, much to my surprise, her husband insisted that their townhouse in London be given to me – and so it has been! I was most astonished and tried to tell them that I would not take it from their possession, but it seems that Lord Armitage desires to purchase a new property here in London and he was determined to assist me." A small sense of relief washed over her again as she recognized the freedom she now had. "The footmen and maids come with it – paid for by Lord Armitage, though I have told him that *I* will pay their wages once I am able to – and he has also given me a carriage and horses. All in all, he is the most generous of gentlemen I think I have ever come across, and I am truly grateful for all he has done."

Lady Guilford leaned a little closer to her, her eyes now glistening.

"I am glad that you have been given such kindness after what you have endured."

Smiling briefly, Jane nodded.

"I have also been given employment, though I do not want you to speak of it to anyone, I beg of you."

"Employment?"

Lady Guilford's voice was so loud, it made Jane wince, though her friend quickly whispered an apology, her cheeks pinking.

"Yes, with The London Chronicle," Jane explained, quietly. "I will have to reply to those seeking advice – and I must tell you, I am already rather overwhelmed at the thought! I do not know if I will be able to give any sort of advice and I fear that I will fail!"

Lady Guilford clicked her tongue.

"I am sure that you will not, you must have a little more confidence in yourself!"

"But might you be willing to help me, should I need it?" Jane asked, a knot of worry tying itself in her stomach as she looked at her friend. "I do feel a little overcome with all manner of thoughts about this employment, I confess it, but to know that I might have someone to turn to would make me feel a good deal better, I am sure."

"Of course you can." Lady Guilford smiled warmly, just as they reached a small group of ladies who were all standing together, though most turned their heads towards Jane and Lady Guilford, a flicker of interest in some of their eyes. "Now come, let me introduce you to some of my acquaintances. You will soon find a great many friends here in London, I am sure of it, and you shall have the most wonderful Season! Without any requirement to find yourself a husband, there is nothing to hold you back from having the very best Season thus far, is there?"

Jane smiled, a gentle swirl of happiness beginning to grow in her chest. In finding Lady Guilford, she had found herself a friend, a support, and a true companion, and that brought a fresh brightness to all she now considered.

"Yes, Louisa, I think that you are right," she agreed, as the ladies nearby broke apart from their small circle so that they might come to join them. "A most wonderful Season indeed."

"A LETTER HAS ARRIVED for you, my Lady."

Jane thanked the butler and took it, at once, from the tray that he held out to her. Looking at it, she expected to see her sister's curved handwriting on the address but, to her surprise, it was not hers at all. Wondering who else would be writing to her, Jane made her way to the drawing room, only for a sudden streak of excitement to rush through her.

The London Chronicle!

Sitting down, she carefully unfolded the letter, only for something to fall out onto her lap. Picking up what appeared to be yet another letter, she set it to one side before reading the first.

'*I am delighted to welcome you to The London Chronicle. Please find enclosed the first letter seeking advice, which we hope you will soon be able to answer. As this is your first response, we would ask for it to be returned to us no later than in three days' time.*'

Jane did not even stop to look at the rest of the letter, setting it aside so that she might pick up the other. Opening it with trembling hands, she closed her eyes for just a moment as she took a long breath, not quite certain that she was prepared for all that was to come. She read it aloud.

'I am writing in the hope that you might offer me some advice since I can get none from those around me. I have a gentleman eager to court me and both my father and mother are encouraging me to accept his courtship, though I myself am a little less than inclined. Instead, there is a second gentleman whom I wish to consider. The first gentleman is known to have an excellent character, and is morally upright and kind-hearted, though he does not have as high a title nor as great a fortune as the second gentleman. The second gentleman, on the other hand, does not have as excellent a character as the first, though I find that I am drawn to the latter rather than the former. My parents are both very good in that they permit me to make my own decisions, though I do feel the pressure of their desires. I look forward to reading what you have to say.'

Jane closed her eyes, her heart aching suddenly for this young lady, whoever she was.

"I do not need three days to respond to this," she murmured to herself, opening her eyes and rising to her feet, suddenly eager to write her response that very moment rather than losing any time. "And I know exactly what to say."

CHAPTER FIVE

"*H*ave you seen The London Chronicle today? Everyone is abuzz with it!"

Oliver looked down at Miss Dutton, seeing the excitement in her expression.

"No, I have not." He chuckled at her disappointment. "I confess that I do not often have time to read such things."

"Oh, but you must!" Miss Dutton exclaimed, putting her arm through his. "Though I will say that there is often rumor within it, which I do not appreciate."

Understanding this, Oliver said nothing but continued meandering through St James Park with the lady on his arm, a little surprised that the park was as quiet as it was. He would have thought that this fine afternoon would have brought many a gentleman and lady to the grounds and, truth be told, he had been rather proud that Miss Dutton had agreed to take a walk with him through the park. Having considered her enthusiasm, and decided that he was being foolish in being uncertain of it, he had told himself to pursue her and thus, he had done so. He had taken tea with her the previous day, and had then asked if she would like to join him for a walk in the park, and had been delighted when she had accepted immediately. Her mother was walking behind them, clearly just as pleased as her daughter had been at Oliver's attentions, and all in all, Oliver felt himself rather pleased with his new connection. Miss Dutton was pretty, enthusiastic, spoke well, and offered great warmth after only a very short acquaintance – and he could not imagine what further would be offered to him should their connection grow to something more!

"Should you like me to tell you what has made the *ton* so intrigued?"

Pulling himself out of his thoughts, Oliver looked back at the lady.

"Yes, of course! I should not like to be the only one in society who does not know of it!"

"Very well, then I shall tell you, so that you are not in the dark," Miss Dutton replied, beaming up at him as though he had offered her some great boon. "There is a new feature in The London Chronicle, you see. Someone writes to the newspaper with a request for advice on whatever situation they find themselves in, and both the letter and the response from the newspaper are printed together, side by side. This time, the letter seeking advice is quite astonishing, speaking of a lady torn between two gentlemen – and the response is also rather surprising! It is fair, yes, but also rather fierce, as though the writer is speaking from experience and that, I think, is what has caught the interest of so many within society."

"I see." For a moment, a flash of thought came to him, wondering what it would be like if he wrote in to the newspaper, seeking advice on how to find the right young lady, though it floated out of his mind very quickly thereafter. He had found a good connection in Miss Dutton, had he not?

He might well have no requirement, then, for writing to the newspaper for advice. "You said that it was firm, however, in its tone? I do wonder if that will be taken well."

"Oh, I should think it would be," Miss Dutton answered, with a firm nod. "The response was very fair in what it said, speaking of understanding over one's heart but how one ought not always to listen to what it is saying! The truth is, I think that the lady who wrote in search of advice was seeking to attach herself to a scoundrel rather than to the sensible gentleman who was hopeful of pursuing her. That, I suppose, I can understand."

A frown played across Oliver's forehead.

"You can?"

What was offered to him by way of response was nothing other than a slightly enigmatic smile, but nothing more, leaving Oliver feeling a little unsettled. Perhaps, he considered, it was simply that all young ladies could find themselves drawn to rogues and scoundrels – for that was precisely what made such gentlemen so! Telling himself that he had no need to be concerned about such a thing, Oliver cleared his throat and offered a smile.

"I am glad that there was good advice offered. I do hope that the young lady takes it."

"As do I."

"Edenbridge?"

Oliver lifted his gaze from Miss Dutton, seeing one of his acquaintances approaching, his eyes a little wide as he looked at Miss Dutton, and then back to Oliver.

"Ah, good afternoon Lord Ravenscourt. The park is rather quiet, is it not? I confess, I am surprised given that–"

"I see that you are walking with Miss Dutton," the gentleman interrupted, his eyes fixed on the lady who, for whatever reason, stuck her chin out as she narrowed her gaze just a little. "I confess, I am surprised. I always thought that you were an upstanding sort."

"I beg your pardon?" Confused and a little slighted by the remark, Oliver drew himself up. "I do not think that walking with one particular lady makes me in the least bit improper, Lord Ravenscourt! As you can see, she is properly chaperoned."

Lord Ravenscourt snorted.

"As though that would account for anything!"

This remark left Oliver in such confusion that he did not know what to say. Clearly, there was something that Lord Ravenscourt knew that he did not, something about Miss Dutton that was troubling him – and something that Oliver had no knowledge of.

"Lord Edenbridge?" Another gentleman came to join them, his eyebrows lifting. "And Miss Dutton? I do declare, I did not think–"

"It seems to me that Lord Edenbridge is a good deal more forgiving than the rest of society."

Miss Dutton's voice broke through the conversation, her hand now tightening on Oliver's arm, though he was beginning to go cold all over, fearful now that he had made some sort of mistake in building his connection with Miss Dutton.

Oliver rubbed one hand over his eyes, wishing now that he could step away from the lady without any sort of difficulty, but her hand was so tight, it felt like a vice.

"I was only taking a walk with the lady, that is all."

"Then you are not... interested in forming a connection with her?"

The urge to say no was strong, but the awareness of how gravely he would hurt Miss Dutton kept those words back. Instead, he became defensive, drawing himself up as he gazed into Lord Ravenscourt's face.

"I hardly think that such questions are proper for any gentleman of the *ton* to be asking another, particularly in public," he said, as firmly as he could, as Lord Ravenscourt's eyebrows lifted. "If you have something you wish to speak to me about, then I would suggest that it is said in private."

Lord Ravenscourt sent a look to the other gentleman, then began to chuckle, though it was not a mirthful sound.

"Then you do not know."

"Know what?" Oliver asked, frowning. "I do not think–"

"You do not know of the scandal involving the lady you are now standing with," the gentleman answered, as a quick glance towards Miss Dutton revealed a flushed face and sharp eyes directed towards Lord Ravenscourt. "I think that you would do well to learn about that just as soon as possible. I–"

"Excuse me? I cannot make my way past."

Oliver turned, a little relieved by the interruption. A lady looked back at him and instantly, a rush of what felt like sparks ran up Oliver's spine and went down over his back. The lady's eyes were as blue as the sky above them, her golden curls dancing lightly in the summer breeze. Her cheeks were a little pink, but it was the soft smile on her lips that caught his attention. She had clearly not overheard any of their conversation, but was seeking simply to walk along the path which they were blocking by the way that they stood. Whether it was her presence or her smile – which was the antithesis of the conversation that Oliver was in the middle of – he did not know, but instantly, he warmed to her.

"Do excuse us," he said, hastily. "We were only just now speaking of a... well, that does not matter. We are in your way and–"

"Lady Jane?"

Miss Dutton's eyes rounded, her hand going to her heart. The lady in question frowned, however, perhaps not recognizing her.

"You are closely acquainted with my sister, Hannah, though she is now Lady Worthing," Miss Dutton continued, only for the other lady's eyes to widen in surprise.

"Oh, of course. Miss Dutton, I... yes, I knew your sister well. I am no longer Lady Jane, however, but Lady Harsham." She did not curtsey, her eyes searching Miss Dutton's face. "Do tell your sister that I send her my regards. I shall not interrupt your conversation any longer, however. I–"

Oliver interrupted suddenly, the words coming out of him before he had even given himself any time to think about what to say.

"Pray do not, Lady Harsham. If you would be so kind as to walk with me for a time, I would be grateful. It seems that Miss Dutton will have to make her way back to her mother now, for our time together has come to an end."

Miss Dutton's shoulders dropped.

"Lord Edenbridge, please do not be so! I have done nothing to you, nothing that should keep you from me."

"Except you have not told him about Lord Soutar," Lord Ravenscourt interrupted, as Oliver's jaw tightened, a mixture of embarrassment and upset burning through him.

"I shall speak with you again at another time, Miss Dutton," he said, as gently as he could, so that she would not be too upset with him and, mayhap, cause yet more people within the park to come to join them. "If you would."

Miss Dutton's eyes narrowed, sparks seeming to spit out at him as she put both hands on her hips.

"I should have known that you would be just as every other gentleman is, here in London," she said, sharply. "I do not think that we need to speak again, Lord Edenbridge, not if you are going to be as judgmental as the rest!"

So saying, she turned on her heel and flounced back toward her mother, leaving Oliver hot with mortification. No doubt Lord Ravenscourt would have every desire to tell others about what had taken place and soon, rumors about him would be spreading all through London.

"Shall we walk?" A gentle, sweet voice made Oliver's heart lift just a little, pulling it away from where it had been sinking low. "I should be glad of some company, for I have no one to walk with today," Lady Harsham continued, her eyes warm with evident sympathy. "What say you, Lord Edenbridge?"

Oliver nodded, then looked at Lord Ravenscourt, seeing that the other gentleman had already taken his leave.

"Do excuse me, Ravenscourt."

The gentleman put one hand on his shoulder, keeping him there.

"You did not know about Miss Dutton? Truly?"

Shaking his head, Oliver shrugged as Lord Ravenscourt dropped his hand.

"I did not. You may call me as foolish as you wish, for that is what I have been, it seems." He did not ask the gentleman to keep what had happened to himself, fully aware that even that sort of request might be used as fodder for the local gossips. "I should be grateful to you for speaking to me as you did. I would not have known otherwise." Lord Ravenscourt's eyes flickered, but he nodded and then, with a quick smile, stepped away. Oliver dropped his head, closed his eyes, and let out a slow breath, only to recall that Lady Harsham was beside him. "Forgive me for pulling you into this most awkward situation," he muttered, glancing at her. "You need not walk with me if you do not wish it. I may as well return to my carriage!"

"If you did so, would you not then find yourself walking again with Miss Dutton and her mother?" Lady Harsham's lips curved gently. "I do not mind in the least walking with you, Lord Edenbridge. We have not been properly acquainted, however, so mayhap we ought to introduce ourselves first."

Oliver nodded, grateful to her for her consideration.

"The Marquess of Edenbridge." He bowed his head. "Thank you for your willingness to show me some kindness. I am grateful."

She smiled again and then dropped into a curtsey.

"Jane, Lady Harsham," she said, quietly.

Married, then. Understanding now why she was able to walk alone and without any chaperone near her, Oliver's spirits lifted a little more.

"How very good to meet you." He began to walk, the lady falling into step beside him. "Have you been in London for long?"

She shook her head.

"I have been in London for only a sennight. Though, I confess, I already knew about Miss Dutton."

"You did?" Oliver stopped walking at once, turning to face her. "Might you tell me about the scandal? I confess that I do not know in the least bit what is wrong! I thought Miss Dutton pleasant, entertaining, and very warm in her conversation and interest in my company." As he spoke, it was as though a heavy cloud settled on his heart, pulling his brows low. "Though, if she has something of a reputation where very few of the *ton* will connect with her, then that might explain her eagerness."

Lady Harsham winced.

"That might be so, I am afraid. Do you wish me to tell you the details?"

Nodding, Oliver let out a slow breath. "I suppose it would be best. I shall not continue my connection with her, of course, but all the same, I should like to know what it is that will, no doubt, shock the *ton* when they hear that I have been walking with her."

With a small sigh, Lady Harsham looked up at him, beginning to walk slowly again.

"The *ton* can be rather difficult, can they not? Though all the same, in this instance, it appears to me that Miss Dutton was the one who behaved improperly. I say this because I have been informed by a close friend that Miss Dutton herself was the one who pursued a gentleman."

"Pursued?" Oliver frowned. "A young lady seeking a match with a particular fellow is not a bad thing, is it?"

A flush crept into Lady Harsham's cheeks.

"I do not mean to say that she sought a match, Lord Edenbridge. It is more that she sought a connection that would not lead to marriage, if you can understand my meaning." Glancing at him, she closed her eyes and laughed though Oliver understood it came from a sense of embarrassment. "It was to be nothing more than a brief connection, I believe. The gentleman, Lord Soutar, claims that it was the lady's doing and not his own, though I am uncertain as to who speaks the truth."

A slight heat pulled into Oliver's chest.

"Ah. I believe I fully understand." He cleared his throat gruffly, looking away from her for fear that his face would grow hot. "That would explain, then, why there was such shock over my connection with the lady, yes? And in addition, it would also explain why she appeared so fervent in her desire to dance with me."

Despite his attempts, he felt that very same heat creep up into his neck and then, into his face. Having no choice but to turn his head back towards her for fear that she would think him rude otherwise, he lifted his shoulders and then let them fall, saying nothing more.

Lady Harsham offered him just a small smile, and the two then walked in silence for some moments. It was not an uncomfortable silence, however, Oliver noticed. Rather, he felt himself slowly beginning to settle inwardly, a growing sense of peace overtaking him. Whether it was the lady's company, he did not know, but all the same, he appreciated it.

"I am sure that the gentlemen speaking with you will have recognized that you did not know the lady" Finally breaking the silence, Lady Harsham stopped, smiled at him, and then gestured to the path which turned to the left. "I think I shall walk this way, Lord Edenbridge. Thank you for your company."

"No, thank you for yours!" Oliver exclaimed, bowing swiftly. "Lady Harsham, I am in your debt. You did not need to come and join me as you did, but in your kindness, you took pity on me and chose to do so. Thank you for that. I think that I would have been quite lost in shame had you not done so! And I must also thank you for your willingness to explain to me about Miss Dutton, something which I would not have fully understood so quickly unless you had spoken so." With a small sigh, he pressed his lips flat and then looked away, a small sigh escaping him. "It seems that I am doomed to failure."

"Failure?" A slight lift of the lady's eyebrow betrayed her curiosity, though Oliver did not want to explain all. He had already burdened her enough, he considered, his lips quirking a little.

"Let me just say that I have found it a little more difficult to find a suitable young lady to court than I had otherwise expected." It was a clear but simple answer, accompanied by another shrug and a wry smile. "But I am sure that, despite the mistakes I have made and the missteps I have taken, I will be successful at some point soon."

Lady Harsham smiled.

"I am sure that you will," she answered, softly. "Though if you are truly in as much difficulty as you state, might I suggest that you consider writing to The London Chronicle? It seems to me as though the advice given to the first letter – printed today – has gone down rather well in society. Mayhap you will find something similar to assist you, also."

Dismissing the idea inwardly, Oliver nodded, smiled, and thanked her for her advice. When she excused herself and turned away, Oliver could not help but watch her leave, thinking silently that Lady Harsham was a very kind lady, one with a sympathetic heart and a gentle spirit.

Her husband must be very fortunate to have her as his wife. The thought came with a hint of sadness in its wake, though Oliver quickly threw it off and, with a silent berating of himself for such foolish thoughts, turned on his heel and walked back towards his carriage.

The afternoon had not ended as dreadfully as it might otherwise have done, and for that, Oliver was very grateful indeed. There was even a slight lift in his step as he made his way through the park and that, he knew, was solely because of Lady Harsham.

CHAPTER SIX

*W*hy ever did I suggest that he write to The London Chronicle?

Jane pushed a strand of hair back behind her ear as she looked through the three letters that had arrived for her to consider. Part of her hoped that Lord Edenbridge had written to her, but the other part of her dreaded it, wondering what she might say to assist him. What had possessed her to suggest such a thing to him, she could not say, but there had been something in his eyes that had made sympathy build within her heart. Yes, he had obviously – and badly – misstepped with Miss Dutton... and that was the second time he had done so, so he had said, and thus, she had felt rather sorry for him. Lord Edenbridge did appear to be a good sort of gentleman, although, she reminded herself, that did not mean that he was. Her husband had not been a good fellow at all, and she had only learned the extent of his dark temper and cruel character once she had been married to him. Reading the second letter, Jane squeezed her eyes closed tight, her lips bunching. This letter, the one which had no name, sounded as though it might well be from Lord Edenbridge – though she had very little idea of what to say in response!

A knock at the door made her start in surprise, having been lost in her thoughts about Lord Edenbridge.

"Yes?"

The butler opened the door.

"Lady Guilford, my Lady."

Jane rose at once.

"A tea tray, if you please." Having directed the butler, she beamed as her friend came into the room, delighted to see her. "Louisa! How good to see you. Why are you here?"

"I came to call!" Lady Guilford sailed into the room, embracing Jane warmly. "You were out walking in the park with a gentleman, I have been told, and I simply must know who it was!"

A flush touched Jane's cheeks as she sat down.

"I suppose I should not be surprised at how quickly the *ton* speaks about such things," she sighed, though Louisa only chuckled softly. "Yes, it is true that I was walking with a gentleman in the park, but I did so only to assist him." Seeing her friend's eyebrows lift, she shook her head. "The gentleman had been walking with a young lady without realizing her reputation."

"Really?" Lady Guilford's eyes opened wide. "Who was she?"

Pausing for a moment and wondering if her friend was going to gossip about this, Jane considered that she would not and, thus, she spoke honestly.

"I know that you will not say anything to anyone, but it was Lord Edenbridge walking with Miss Dutton."

"Oh." Lady Guilford shook her head. "I am surprised that Lord Edenbridge did not know."

"You are acquainted with him, then?"

Lady Guilford shook her head.

"Not particularly well, though we have been introduced. All the same, it is unusual for a gentleman of the *ton* not to know about what has been happening with such things as that."

Jane shrugged.

"Mayhap he is disinclined towards gossip."

"Mayhap."

The tea tray was brought in, and Jane refrained from conversation until the maid had left the room, going on, then, to pour the tea. Once they were both settled with tea, she gestured to the three letters beside her.

"I have just now received the next few letters sent to The London Chronicle."

Lady Guilford's expression brightened.

"That is wonderful! I thought your first response was quite perfect."

"Did you?" Jane smiled at her. "I must say, I was greatly relieved to see that the *ton* thought it quite acceptable. I was concerned that some would not agree with what I said."

"Nonsense! You answered very well, though I know it was from experience that you spoke, and I am sorry for that." Lady Guilford smiled a little sadly. "Let us hope that the lady in question, whoever she is, takes on your advice!" Her gaze went to the letters as Jane nodded. "Might you wish to tell me what these letters contain?"

Jane picked up the first one.

"I confess that I am a little uncertain as to which I ought to reply to first, though I do think that one is quite useless and does not require a reply."

"Oh?"

With a quiet laugh, Jane picked up the offending letter and read it aloud.

'To Whom It May Concern, might I enquire as to who it is that writes your responses to these letters? Though I will not disagree that the reply to the young lady seeking advice was very well given, I do think that I might have given a little more to her. Therefore, should you be seeking someone new to write these responses – or, indeed, a response to go alongside the other, then might I suggest you consider me?'

Setting the letter down, Jane laughed aloud as her friend shook her head in clear astonishment, though she was smiling.

"It is quite extraordinary, is it not?"

"It is." A gleam came into Lady Guilford's eye. "Might I enquire as to who it is that has written it?"

Jane hesitated, letting her eyes narrow in a friendly, teasing manner.

"You may - though you must promise me that you will not speak of this to anyone, my dear friend. You know that you cannot breathe a word about my employment to anyone, yes?"

A slight flash of hurt dashed across Lady Guilford's expression and Jane was about to instantly apologize, only for her friend to shrug.

"I suppose you are wise to be reminding me of my responsibility towards you, and the secrecy that you have about this position," she said, with a slightly wry smile. "I confess to you that I do somewhat enjoy hearing society's gossip, though I do my best not to share it." Putting one hand to her heart, Lady Guilford looked at Jane directly. "I promise you, I shall not say a single word of this to anyone."

Jane smiled.

"I thank you."

Handing the letter to her friend, she waited for Lady

Guilford's response, only to burst into laughter when Lady Guilford let out a shriek of astonishment.

"Lord Hedley?" she exclaimed, as Jane nodded, knowing all too well who Lord Hedley was.

Something of a fop, he seemed to pride himself on being the very center of attention wherever he went, preening himself as though he were a magnificent bird who wanted to appear at his very best on any occasion.

"I did not at first think it was from a gentleman, I confess it!" Jane chuckled as her friend shook her head. "I thought it might be a lady seeking to usurp me from my position."

"But it was not! Good gracious, no doubt he would want everyone to know that it was he who offered his advice rather than keeping it anonymous, as you do."

"Though," Jane countered, wincing as she spoke, "I did suggest to Lord Edenbridge that he write to The London Chronicle seeking advice for his present situation." Holding up one hand, palm out, to silence the questions before they began, Jane shook her head. "No, I do not know why I suggested that he do so, and I certainly have no thought as to what I should say to him, but..." Gesturing to one of the other letters, she let out a sigh. "I believe that this anonymous letter is from him."

"Then read it!" Lady Guilford exclaimed, flapping one hand at her. "I will pour more tea for I am certain that we will need some more to fortify us!"

Appreciating her friend's consideration, Jane paused for a moment and then began to read.

'I have found myself seeking a bride this Season. However, circumstances mean that I am not considered as favorably as I had hoped, and even with that, I have not managed to secure a young lady's attention. On the few occasions I have been successful, I have been met with what we shall call 'difficulties', though I shall not go into any more detail than that. If you have any sort of advice that you might wish to offer a gentleman in seeking out a kind, considerate, and charming young lady for his bride, I should be very glad to hear of it, for I find myself in the doldrums on this matter and fear I might soon give up entirely.'

Finishing, she looked up at Lady Guilford, only to see her friend's sad expression, one hand now pressed lightly to her heart.

"How very sad, if it is he," Lady Guilford said, softly. "Lord Edenbridge is an excellent gentleman, I am sure, for there has never been any whisper of disrepute about him."

"That is good for me to hear, although I am then a little confused as to why, then, he is not looked upon favorably by the *ton*."

Her friend tilted her head.

"There was concern over his fortune, I recall." A pink touched her cheeks as she glanced away, perhaps a little embarrassed, Jane considered, at revealing yet more gossip. "From what I know, his late father was very foolish with some of his investments and did, I think, lose a great deal of his fortune. All of society knew of it, for it was not hidden from anyone thanks to one gossiping solicitor, I am afraid."

"Oh." Jane's heart twisted all the more with a sharp sympathy. "Then this letter must be from him, I am sure of it."

"And shall you answer it?"

Hesitating, Jane looked down at the letter again.

"I confess, I do not know what to say! It seems to me that it is not his fault that he made a mistake with Miss Dutton, it is simply that he did not listen to gossip, which is no bad thing. It also appears, from what you have said, that his lack of fortune does not, again, come from his own fool-ishness or the like. It has been a difficulty placed upon his shoulders, which he has had to bear. I am sure that he has done all that he can to improve the situation however, though it may be that he seeks a wife to garner a large dowry." Something tightened in her chest, though Jane did not know why. "Perhaps he is seeking a good deal of money from his bride, in which case, I–"

"No, that cannot be." Sounding quite determined, Lady Guilford shook her head. "Miss Dutton does not have a large dowry, I am sure of it. Her father is a Viscount and a rather poor one at that, so even though a large dowry might have attracted her a husband after all she has done, I would be very surprised if he was able to promise that for her."

Jane considered this, nodding slowly.

"Very well. Then he seeks a wife only because he desires one."

"And she must be kind and considerate, yes?" Lady Guilford smiled. "It seems to me as though his desire is genuine, for he truly wishes to have a lady of good character as his bride. It matters to him what the lady's heart is like, rather than simply being contented to marry a lady of high standing in society."

For whatever reason, Jane let her thoughts drift back to when she had been walking with Lord Edenbridge. Instead of responding to her friend, she thought about Lord Eden-bridge's frustration, his upset and embarrassment during the conversation with the two gentlemen and Miss Dutton herself – as well as how those emotions had faded away when he had begun to walk with her. His brown eyes, which had been dark with emotion, had slowly begun to lighten and the heaviness of his frame had seemed to lift as they had walked. He was, she considered, a handsome gentleman though that did not seem to matter to the ladies of the *ton* for, if there were questions about his fortune, then many of them would be dissuaded from even considering him.

"Jane?"

Blinking quickly, Jane looked back at Lady Guilford, seeing her slight smile.

"Yes?"

"What is it that you are going to write?"

"I – I do not know." A little helpless, Jane spread out her hands. "What am I to write to a gentleman like him? A gentleman who has nothing wrong about him, aside from the fact that there are those who are uncertain over his fortune."

"And those who will, no doubt, soon be whispering about his connection to Miss Dutton which will, unfortunately, damage his reputation somewhat." With a slight shake of her head, Lady Guilford sighed. "I shall not say anything, of course, but his interest in the lady will have captured the attention of some."

"Then I shall try to be as encouraging as I can," Jane decided, a sudden determination sweeping through her. "I shall inform him that the right young lady will not care about his fortune, that he must continue simply to be the very best sort of gentleman he can and prove his character that way."

Lady Guilford smiled.

"I think that an excellent idea though, however, I would suggest that you also give him a practical action, if you might. Something that will spur him on, something that he can take a hold of and enact."

Biting her lip, Jane tried to think of what that could be.

"It has been so long since I have been in society that I cannot think of what to suggest."

"I am sure that you will," came the reply, as her friend rose from her chair. "No, I shall not tell you what it is that you should write, for I can see that hope in your eyes, but I cannot fulfill it. You have the ability, I know. You must only believe that you do."

Jane rose to her feet quickly, desperation and a sprinkling of fear in her chest.

"I do not have the same confidence in my ability as you do, Louisa. What if you are wrong? What if I cannot find the right thing to say?"

Lady Guilford smiled, reached out, and squeezed Jane's hand.

"Write from your heart, my dear friend, and I can assure you, every word will be quite perfect. I know it."

CHAPTER SEVEN

*O*liver scowled at his friend.

"You did not need to ask me such a thing so loudly!"

Lord Dunstable had the grace to look embarrassed.

"Forgive me. I did not think. Besides, this ballroom is so noisy, I was quite sure that no one would overhear and though that is not an excuse, I do not think that you are in any sort of danger of being discovered."

The scowl on Oliver's face dug in a little more deeply.

"All the same, there is the chance."

When Lord Dunstable had asked him – in a very loud voice – whether he had read the letter in The London Chronicle, or if he had no need to because he had been the one to write it – Oliver had not known what to do or what to say. He had been standing alone at the time, but there had been others near him, and he had been sure that the occasional glances sent in his direction had been because of Lord Dunstable's question.

"I am truly sorry, I did not think." Lord Dunstable offered Oliver a small smile but, even then, Oliver's spirits did not lift. "Though you did not answer my question, I notice."

"That is because I was attempting to remove myself from the situation without being required to answer," Oliver replied, grimly. "Goodness, the last thing I need is to have the *ton* speak of me even more than they already are!"

Lord Dunstable set one hand on Oliver's shoulder, stopping him.

"My deepest apologies, my friend."

Closing his eyes, Oliver nodded a little stiffly.

"I thank you."

"And I do not believe that you are in any sort of danger... at least, not about that," his friend continued, wincing when Oliver frowned. "Yes, the *ton* have been speaking about your connection to Miss Dutton, though given that there are also whispers about Lord Kettering, I am sure it will pass through society very quickly."

"Lord Kettering?"

Lord Dunstable nodded.

"It appears that he has become quite the scoundrel! Though," he continued, a glint in his eye. "Might you now be willing to answer my question? Did you write that letter to The London Chronicle?"

Looking away, Oliver gave a somewhat terse nod.

"It was Lady Harsham who suggested it," he said, a trifle heavily. "No doubt she may also have been speaking of my foolishness to her friends and yet more rumors will have followed after her words! But yes, I do confess that I spoke a little more openly to her than might have been wise, but I could not seem to help it. She was very willing to listen, and her gentle manner was encouraging to me. Though now, I think, I will need to be a good deal more careful in what I say to Lady Harsham, for fear that she will take what I have said and speak of it to others."

"I can assure you, I will not."

Oliver's whole body went cold as he slowly turned around to see none other than the very lady whom he had been speaking of, sitting in a chair just behind him. Her blue eyes were cold, pushing sharp needles of guilt into his chest as she gazed up at him, her hands clasped together in her lap.

"Lady Harsham, good evening." It was Lord Dunstable who spoke first, bowing low and then offering the lady a small smile. "Forgive us both, we did not see you there."

"I am well aware of that, otherwise I do not think you would have spoken of me in such a way," came the answer, making Oliver's face grow hot. "Though I should like to reassure you, Lord Edenbridge, that I will not ever speak a word of what you shared with me to anyone. I am not in the habit of gossiping, despite what you might think, and I have no interest in sharing what was a private conversation."

Oliver put one hand to his heart and inclined his head, the embarrassment still burning through him.

"I am terribly sorry, Lady Harsham. Our acquaintance has been brief and, I confess, I assumed that you were very much like every other young lady of my acquaintance."

Something changed in Lady Harsham's expression, and she rose to her feet.

"I think I can understand that and, on this occasion, offer you some mercy instead."

A tiny smile touched the corners of her lips, and her sharp gaze softened, making Oliver feel as though he could breathe a little more easily again.

"I thank you. You are most kind."

"Indeed, you are," Lord Dunstable agreed, smiling at

the lady. "It is good to see you again, Lady Harsham, though I confess that it has been some time since we were first acquainted. Mayhap you have forgotten – I am the Earl of Dunstable."

A streak of what felt like red hot heat rushed up Oliver's spine, though he could not explain why.

"Lord Dunstable is my closest friend," he said, as his friend bowed.

"Though I was just now being berated for some foolishness on my part," Lord Dunstable added, making Lady Harsham smile brightly. "Foolishness which I have admitted to and now regret." He tilted his head before Oliver could say a word. "Might I ask if you have read The London Chronicle today? All of the *ton* are speaking of the letter written, and the advice which has been given."

A flicker came into Lady Harsham's eyes, though her expression did not change. Was it curiosity? An awareness of what Lord Dunstable was speaking of? Butterflies began to flit around his stomach, though he told himself that Lord Dunstable would never inform the lady herself that Oliver had been the letter-writer.

"What did you think of the advice?" Lady Harsham's eyes searched Oliver's face before returning to Lord Dunstable. "It was brief, was it not?"

"Brief, yes but succinct," Oliver spoke quickly, not daring to look at Lord Dunstable for fear that something in that would give him away to Lady Harsham. "The encouragement to be the very best gentleman he could be is excellent advice, for it is indeed the character of the gentleman – or the lady, of course – which matters the most, is it not?"

Lady Harsham's smile crept upwards.

"Yes, I quite agree."

"Though the practical instruction was certainly inter-

THE TRUTH ABOUT THE MARQUESS | 71

esting," Lord Dunstable added, making Lady Harsham's eyebrows lift. "The suggestion to only consider three young ladies at any one time was not something which I would have said."

"No?"

The question lingered in the air between them all as Lord Dunstable considered.

"No," Lord Dunstable confirmed, after a moment. "I might have suggested to a gentleman that he considers a good many more than that, only to then *narrow* the selection if you understand me."

"Though I think it a good suggestion," Oliver interrupted, seeing how Lady Harsham's eyebrows leaped up just a little. "To consider only three means that the gentleman, whoever he is, will not become distracted by the many names and faces that surround him. It is clear to me that he is a gentleman who is looking for a young lady with specific qualities and to throw the net wide, as you might say, could lead to a great struggle and no clear path. He could find himself exasperated rather than contented!"

"I am glad to hear you say so." Lady Harsham flushed, then dropped her head for just a moment. "Forgive me, I mean to say that my opinion aligns with yours, Lord Edenbridge, and thus I do now feel a little relieved that I am not alone in my thoughts."

"But of course." Smiling at her, Oliver paused, then held out one hand, hearing the next dance being called. "Lady Harsham, might I ask if you would like to dance?" Realizing that he had not yet asked to be introduced to Lord Harsham, Oliver cleared his throat. "Only if your husband is contented with you stepping out with another gentleman, of course."

Lady Harsham's eyebrows shot up, her eyes fixing to his.

"Oh, Lord Edenbridge, I thought I had already told you, so you must forgive me if I have not. My husband passed away nearly two years ago now."

"Oh." Mortification swirled through him as he began to question whether or not she had already told him, and he had not been listening to her as she had done so. "I am terribly sorry – both to hear that from you and also for my lack of awareness. Perhaps you already told me and–"

"No, I am sure that I did not." Lady Harsham smiled and then took his hand, rendering Oliver silent as shock – or was it relief? – rushed through him. "Yes, I should be glad to dance, I thank you."

It was not until Lord Dunstable cleared his throat that Oliver started and then responded, going cold and then hot again as he realized that he had been standing staring at the lady for the last few minutes.

"Forgive me, I was lost in confusion for a moment."

He smiled and then, lifting her hand in his, turned and walked towards the center of the chalked floor, ready to dance the cotillion with the lady.

They did not say much to each other as they danced, though Oliver found that there was no awkwardness there, no pressure upon him to find the right words to speak. Instead, he enjoyed her smiles, the few words that they did share, and with it, the relief that came in knowing that she did not hold his harsh words about her against him.

When the dance came to an end, Oliver offered the lady his arm.

"Might I find you some refreshment, Lady Harsham?"

She tipped her head, just a little.

"I should like to accept, but I would not like to prevent

you from seeking out any young ladies, Lord Edenbridge. Three, was not the advice?"

Astonishment ran through him as he stared back at her, only for the lady to drop her gaze, her face turning a slow shade of pink.

"How... how did you know that I had written that letter?"

Lady Harsham closed her eyes and then pressed her lips together, as though she were preparing to give him an explanation, but struggling to find the words, only for a clear realization to strike itself across Oliver's heart. With a groan, he shook his head, rubbing one hand over his eyes.

"Of course. You overheard my conversation with Lord Dunstable. Forgive me, I did not realize."

"I – I should not have been eavesdropping," the lady began, only for Oliver to shake his head.

"No, no. It was myself and Lord Dunstable who were speaking without any real consideration for who might be around us. I believe that I thought, in approaching a quieter part of the ballroom, that there would be no one to hear us, but that was a foolish thought, was it not?" He let out a wry chuckle, then shrugged. "I suppose there is no need for me to pretend any longer. Yes, Lady Harsham, I took your advice, and I wrote to The London Chronicle." He offered his arm again and this time, much to his relief, she took it, and they began to walk together. "I am sure that you already suspected that I was the one who wrote that letter, after what you had witnessed between myself and Miss Dutton, and our conversation thereafter."

A tinkling laugh came from Lady Harsham, though her cheeks were still hot.

"Yes, I confess that I was."

"Then I confirmed it in what I said," Oliver continued,

with another rueful smile. "I do hope that you do not think me foolish, Lady Harsham. I do have specific... *requirements,* but I do not think that a bad thing."

"No indeed! I think it an excellent notion," came the reply, as Lady Harsham smiled warmly up at him. "It is always important to know the true nature of the person you might soon marry." Her smile slipped, a flash of some emotion that Oliver could not make out coming into her eyes. "You are wise to be so considered."

"I thank you."

"And you can be assured that I will not speak of what I know to anyone," she continued, as they stopped by a table, picking up a glass each, though Lady Harsham did take her other hand from his arm, separating them. She took a sip though her eyes did not leave his, as though she was considering something but not quite certain whether or not to say it.

Oliver waited, keeping a small smile fixed on his lips.

"I could..." Lady Harsham sighed and looked away. "I could assist you if you wish. I may not be any help since I have been out of society for so long, but I could certainly find out a little more about the characters of the young ladies you might consider a good deal more easily than you could."

A surge of hope rushed through Oliver, making him beam back at her.

"That would be both welcome and wonderful, Lady Harsham!"

She looked surprised, perhaps having expected him to refuse her.

"Are you quite sure? As I have said, I might be of very little use."

"But I trust you," he said, realizing that he did, in fact,

trust the lady's word, even after such a short acquaintance. "You seem to understand what it is that I am searching for, and why I seek it so fervently and that, in turn, speaks to my heart. Yes, Lady Harsham, I would be grateful for any help that you can offer me."

"Though I do think that you should still write to The London Chronicle if you wish for more advice," she continued, speaking a little more quietly now, so as not to be overheard. "The advice you have been given seems to have been what you were hoping for and, though I can now help you as you search for the three young ladies to consider, I cannot offer much more than that."

Oliver grinned, his shoulders straightening as a strong hope swept over him.

"I am a good deal more optimistic than I think I have ever been!" he declared, seeing her smile back at him. "With your assistance, with Lord Dunstable's support, and The London Chronicle's writer, I am *certain* to achieve success this Season. I am sure of it."

"I do hope so," came the reply as Lady Harsham lifted her glass in a toast to his success. "By the end of the Season, may you be betrothed to the young lady you have always hoped for."

CHAPTER EIGHT

*J*ane closed her eyes and let out a long, slow breath. The questions that arose in her mind, she quietened one by one, telling herself that she had considered her response and had written not one but three responses, with the third response the most satisfactory.

"This gentleman will know my opinion on his behavior," she murmured, opening her eyes and looking down at what she had written. The letter she had received today had come from a gentleman, albeit a young fellow, she presumed. He sought advice from her, stating that there were those in his company who were encouraging him towards doing nothing other than enjoying himself this Season in all manner of ways, while others were suggesting that he behave as well as he ought. The latter were called dull and staid and foolish by the former gentlemen, and thus, this young fellow found himself torn between two lots of acquaintances and friends.

Jane's words were not sweet nor kind nor considerate. Instead, she had been direct and firm, telling him precisely that the first advice he had been given must have come from the most selfish, arrogant, and inconsiderate gentlemen in all of London and then questioning whether that was the sort of fellow he wished to become. Yes, her words were sharp on occasion but if she could prevent this fellow from becoming yet another rogue or scoundrel within society, then that would satisfy her. That, she considered, was the last thing that the *ton* required – and she had said as much.

"Good afternoon, my dear friend. Are you quite ready?"

Jane turned, just as Lady Guilford walked into the room. Having already informed the butler that she was to let the lady into the house at any time, she smiled and then nodded.

"I am. This play does sound very interesting indeed, though I must quickly seal this letter before we go."

She caught the flash of interest in her friend's eyes as she turned to seal the letter with wax, though she concentrated on that rather than on answering her friend's unspoken questions. Ringing the bell, she smiled at Lady Guilford as she waited for the footman, though she still said nothing.

"You are not going to tell me anything about this, are you?"

Handing the letter to the footman with strict instructions to have it delivered at once, Jane arched an eyebrow as she looked back at her friend.

"I cannot tell you everything that I have received or that I write," she answered, as Lady Guilford chuckled. "You shall have to wait until it is printed come the morrow. Did you know that what I write has become so popular, it is now given an entire page rather than a mere corner? I have had to respond to three letters today and two yesterday!"

"And were there any more from Lord Edenbridge?"

"I do not think it would be right to tell you," Jane teased, aware of the slight tug in her heart. "Even in speaking of him, I confess I feel a great deal of sympathy."

"Sympathy? Still?"

As they walked to the front door and then into Lady Guilford's carriage, her question hung between them, waiting for Jane's answer. It was not until she was seated and the carriage rolling along towards the theatre that Jane answered.

"Yes, I have a great deal of sympathy for him, still. I have seen – or rather, I have heard – his distrust of the *ton* and I can well understand why that is. He has so many people speaking of him and speaking unfairly, that, there is almost no hope left for him to secure a good match. Which is why I have offered to help him."

She winced inwardly, waiting for the explosion of a response that she expected from Lady Guilford, but nothing came from her other than silence. Indeed, it was some minutes before her friend responded and, when she did, it was with a softness about her voice.

"You have always been very kindhearted, Jane." Lady Guilford reached across and patted Jane's hand. "Did you tell him that you were writing the letters back to him?"

Jane shook her head, relieved that Lady Guilford had not expressed great astonishment over what she had chosen to do.

"No, I did not. I said that I might be able to find out a little more about the characters and qualities of the three young ladies he will choose at the first," she said, by way of explanation. "Recall that, in the letter, I did encourage him to consider only three young ladies at any one time."

"I do remember, and I thought it good advice. Though I

must wonder if you are able to keep your two roles separate."

A frown dug into Jane's forehead.

"What do you mean?"

"I mean that I do not understand why you do not simply tell him that you are also writing letters to him in The London Chronicle, if you are going to also be assisting him in other, more practical ways." Lady Guilford tilted her head, her gaze searching. "If you do not tell him the truth now, then you may find yourself accidentally giving yourself away and causing both confusion and, mayhap, some hurt."

Considering this, Jane shook her head.

"I do value your opinion, but I do not think that I want to tell him, not as yet. It may be that my advice is not needed for long, and then all will be well."

Lady Guilford sighed and shook her head.

"I do not think that it is wise but, all the same, I understand. Now, let us talk about other things. Do you think the play will be enjoyable this evening? I confess to knowing very little about it!"

"It is a comedy, and I am very much looking forward to laughing," Jane answered, with a smile. "It is sure to be just the thing I need."

MAKING her way through the crowd, glass in hand, Jane tried not to get lost in the crush. The first half of the play had been most enjoyable, and she had laughed aloud on many occasions, finding herself smiling at just how freely she was able to enjoy the spectacle.

That had not always been the case. Her late husband

had made certain that she was kept away from any sort of frivolity, truth be told, and that had meant a life of sadness and loneliness. Aside from his company, she had not been permitted anyone else to speak with, but now, how much had changed!

"Lady Harsham, how *good* to see you in London." A hand caught her wrist, though it dropped away quickly as Jane turned. "Though I was sorry to hear of the passing of your late husband, of course."

"Of course," Jane murmured, trying to place the lady in front of her. "Your sympathy is much appreciated."

The older lady's smile grew a little fixed, as though, somehow, she knew that Jane did not remember her.

"Might I ask if you are here in London for any particular reason? After all, it has been some time since your husband passed away, has it not?"

Completely taken aback at the lady's blunt question – and aware that there were two other ladies standing with her – it took Jane a moment to answer.

"I confess that I have come here merely to enjoy good company."

"I see."

"Goodness, you are most inquisitive, Lady Marchfield!" One of the other ladies who stood with them trilled a laugh and then waved a hand in Jane's direction, as though to dismiss the concern that Jane now felt. "You must forgive her, she is always so interested in the lives of others – though not in a bad way, you understand. It is out of kindness and consideration."

Jane forced a smile.

"I see."

"I *always* wish to know what I ought to be enquiring after," Lady Marchfield exclaimed, as though she was not truly seeking out gossip, which was what Jane silently believed. "It means that I can show a true care and consideration for each of my acquaintances."

Catching a look shared between the other ladies, one that spoke of utter disbelief in that regard, Jane kept her smile fixed in place.

"That is most considerate, Lady Marchfield. However, I am afraid that there is nothing more for me to say other than to state that I am here in London to find the company I have sorely been lacking these last few years."

Lady Marchfield sniffed.

"Yes, you were quite far removed, were you not?" Jane nodded but said nothing more. "I did not think your husband a particularly good man," Lady Marchfield continued, speaking so plainly and without even a second of consideration as to who else might be listening, or how Jane herself might be feeling about what had been said. "We all know that your marriage was not one of your own choosing, however, for it was your father's agreement, was it not?"

Opening her mouth, Jane found it suddenly dry, struggling to know what to say and how to say it without sounding very rude indeed. She wanted to tell Lady Marchfield that her marriage to Lord Harsham was none of her business whatsoever and that she did not appreciate it being spoken of in such a way... but nothing came to her lips.

"Ah, Lady Harsham, there you are. I see that you have a glass in your hand already, otherwise I would have offered to fetch you one." A smiling face entered the conversation and immediately, Jane's upset began to fade. "I would be glad to accompany you back to your seat. Lady Guilford sent me to find you, you see. I think she quite lost you in the crowd!"

Taking in a deep breath, Jane nodded, her throat constricting just a little.

"Lord Edenbridge, good evening." She managed to smile as relief began to wash through her. "How *very* good it is to see you."

CHAPTER NINE

*L*ady Harsham had not been on Oliver's mind in the least, not until he had spied her coming into the theatre alongside Lady Guilford. He had not been able to explain it even to himself, but something about the lady had drawn his attention, and he had watched her seat herself in the theatre box, ready for the play. Promising himself that he would go and speak with her during the intermission, Oliver had not been able to stop himself from glancing at her now and again as the play had commenced, finding that her bright smile, her sparkling eyes and the clear delight she took in watching the play made him smile also.

Thereafter, however, he had forced himself to consider the young ladies near him and deliberately ensured that his attention remained away from Lady Harsham. After all, his task was now to find three young ladies to consider with a more serious eye, and that was his sole purpose in attending the theatre this evening. Now, wandering through the crowd – all of whom were enjoying both a drink and good conversation – Oliver let his gaze rest on every young lady's face for just a moment, wondering whom he might choose. He had already spoken with one Lady Henrietta – an acquaintance of Lord Dunstable – and that conversation had gone rather well – though he still had two young ladies to find.

"Miss Olivia Leverton," he murmured to himself, spying the young lady as she spoke to another gentleman, though her mother kept a watchful eye upon the conversation. With a nod, he made his way towards her, knowing from previous acquaintance that, though the lady was quiet and a little reserved, he had enjoyed conversation with her last Season. Perhaps it was her shy nature that had not yet brought her a husband.

"Good evening, Lady Keswick, Miss Leverton." He bowed to them both, just as the other gentleman stepped away, which encouraged Oliver all the more. "I do hope that you have both been enjoying the play thus far?"

Miss Leverton looked at her mother first before she spoke, though she then kept her gaze fixed on the floor rather than looking at him, her face coloring slowly.

"Yes, we are. Very much."

"And you, Lord Edenbridge?" Lady Keswick asked, in a voice which was louder than her daughter's. "Have you found it enjoyable?"

Oliver nodded and smiled warmly, hoping that his manner might encourage Miss Leverton to speak more easily and, at the very least, look at him!

"Have you been in London for long?"

Again, Miss Leverton looked at her mother who nodded slowly, as though giving her permission to speak.

"We have been in London for a little over a fortnight," she answered, her voice thin and quiet. "I have been glad to return to good company."

"As have I, I confess it, though I have been sorry to hear of some of the rumors that have been running through society," Oliver answered, hoping that what he said would be construed correctly. "That has always been a disappointment to me. I would have hoped that those in the *ton* would be less inclined towards speaking untruths simply for the enjoyment of it but, alas, it seems that nothing has changed." He cleared his throat as mother and daughter glanced at one another, realizing that he had, most likely, lingered on the point a little too heavily. "Regardless, I am sure that this Season will be quite wonderful." Smiling, he looked directly at Miss Leverton. "I think I should like to call upon you one day soon, Miss Leverton. What say you to that?"

Miss Leverton did not smile, though a brightness instantly came into her mother's expression, her eyes alight as though she was somehow thrilled at this suggestion. Surely, Oliver considered, there had been many gentlemen seeking to do such a thing, for it was very common indeed for gentlemen to call on ladies, even those that they had no intention of pursuing.

"I should be glad to welcome you into our home whenever you wish to call, Lord Edenbridge!" Lady Keswick was the one to answer, her hand going out to grasp Oliver's arm lightly for just a moment. "How very kind you are to think of my dear Olivia."

Oliver kept his smile in place but looked again to Miss Leverton who, he noticed, now hung her head as though she were ashamed – though what she could be ashamed of, he did not know.

"Only if your daughter wishes me to call, Lady Keswick. I would not like her to be put out by my company."

Lady Keswick's eyes gleamed.

"Olivia?"

There was a tightness in the lady's voice, and it instantly lifted Miss Leverton's head, though she still did not smile.

"But of course, Lord Edenbridge, you are very kind."

"Then I shall call at some time this week," Oliver said, still a little confused as to the lady's demeanor. "If that is suitable, of course."

"We shall be glad to see you at any time on any day!" Lady Keswick now sounded almost jubilant, making Oliver's confusion build all the more. "My daughter is a little shy, you understand, and so many gentlemen consider her a wallflower and give her none of their attention – though it seems that you are not one of those gentlemen, Lord Edenbridge!"

Oliver continued to smile uncomfortably, until, nearby, there came a voice.

"I did not think your husband a particularly good man."

The sharp, shrill voice interrupted Oliver's conversation and he turned his head instinctively. Much to his astonishment, he saw Lady Harsham standing opposite him amongst a small group of ladies, though the one who had spoken so bluntly, he did not recognize.

"Lord Edenbridge?"

He turned his head sharply again, catching the way that Lady Keswick's eyes widened.

"Forgive me," he said, his attention still on Lady Harsham and the conversation there. "Yes, of course. I quite understand but I am not as other gentlemen in that regard."

Behind him, distractingly, that sharp voice came again.

"We all know that your marriage was not one of your

own choosing, however, for it was your father's agreement, was it not?"

The conversation involving Lady Harsham dragged him towards it all the more as he overheard the lady's frank remarks and, already imagining what it was that Lady Harsham herself must be feeling, Oliver inclined his head to Lady Keswick and Miss Leverton.

"I shall call very soon. Do excuse me."

Without waiting for either lady to respond, Oliver turned on his heel and made his way directly towards Lady Harsham. She was looking at the lady who had been speaking, a stunned expression on her face and, at once, Oliver interrupted them all.

"Ah, Lady Harsham, there you are. I see that you have a glass in your hand already, otherwise I would have offered to fetch you one." He smiled as warmly as he could, but looked only at her, hoping that he had not overstepped and spoken when he ought to have left her to the conversation. "I would be glad to accompany you back to your seat. Lady Guilford sent me to find you, you see. I think she quite lost you in the crowd!"

Much to his relief, Lady Harsham gave him a small nod, a hint of a smile at her lips, the shock on her face fading.

"Lord Edenbridge, good evening. How *very* good it is to see you."

"You must excuse me for interrupting your conversation," Oliver replied, looking around at the other ladies. "I do believe that the play is soon to start again, however, so mayhap my interruption will not be taken as too dreadful a thing!"

One of the other ladies – one he knew to be Lady Wincott – laughed softly and, relieved, Oliver offered his arm to Lady Harsham.

"I thank you, Lord Edenbridge, for coming in search of me. I was telling Lady Guilford before I came through for the interval, that I thought the play the most excellent thing I have seen in some time! She knows how much I enjoyed it and will have wanted to make certain that I do not miss even a moment of it." She inclined her head. "Good evening to you all. I hope you find the second half of the play to your liking."

"I am sure we shall," Lady Wincott said, before too turning to take her leave. The moment Oliver had Lady Harsham's hand on his arm, however, he led her away from the group as quickly as he could, heedless as to where they were going.

"Thank you, Lord Edenbridge." Lady Harsham looked up at him, her eyes bright with all manner of emotions, though she was not smiling. "I presume you heard a little of what was being said to me?"

Oliver nodded.

"I was in conversation near you, and heard some of the questions that were being asked. I must say, I was not only astonished, I was shocked by the lady's brazenness."

Lady Harsham grimaced.

"Indeed. I was so overcome that I did not manage to form a single sentence by way of answer, which is why I was all the more relieved by your interruption." She set her other hand on his arm, pausing in her walk and turning to look up at him a little more. "I am truly grateful. The *ton* is, no doubt, fully aware of my late husband's character but I did not think that, so long after his passing, there would be such questions!" Oliver said nothing, thinking silently to himself that *he* did not know anything about the late Lord Harsham nor did he have any desire to ask. From what had been said in that brief conversation he had overheard, it seemed to him that the gentleman had been of a somewhat selfish disposition and had certainly not been well thought of. To know that Lady Harsham's father had arranged the match filled his heart with sorrow for her, wondering what it must have been like to hear that the arrangement had been made while, at the same time, knowing there was nothing she could do about it. "You do not know."

The softness of her voice caught him by surprise, and he looked at her.

"No, I do not. I confess. I have been so caught up with remedying my lack of fortune, and with my late father's poor investments, I have not had time for gossip." His lips quirked ruefully. "Not that I have much time for such things in any case. But no, you do not need to tell me about him, I assure you. It is not something that I have any desire to learn about. Your past is your own, just as mine is my own, and we speak of what we desire to speak of, nothing more."

Lady Harsham's eyes grew gentle and for a moment, Oliver was quite lost in them. The room seemed to fade away, the voices growing faint and even the caller announcing that the second half of the play was about to begin grew very quiet indeed.

"Thank you, Lord Edenbridge." Lady Harsham closed her eyes for a moment, pressed his arm, and then let out a small sigh. "I am sure that whichever young lady you decide upon will find themselves quite enthralled by you, once they learn your character." She tipped her head and let out a quiet laugh and the moment faded. "Tell me, have you found any to consider?"

"I have, I think." Oliver smiled as Lady Harsham's eyebrows lifted. "Two, in fact! Though quite what I am to do next now that I have two that I am to consider, I do not know."

Lady Harsham chuckled softly.

"I presume that you are meant to get to know them a little better at the first, that is all."

"Mayhap." A slight worry began to niggle at his heart. "I might write again to The London Chronicle."

At this, Lady Harsham's eyebrows jumped even higher.

"You would seek out the advice from their writer again, over something so simple?"

A flush of heat rose in Oliver's chest and made its way up to his neck.

"I know I might seem a little ridiculous, but you do not know how afraid I am of making yet another mistake!"

"Another mistake in your pursuit of the young ladies of London?" Lady Harsham shook her head. "From what I understand of the situation with Miss Dutton, it was not as though that was your fault. You simply did not know the rumors about her."

"But before that, I thought to pursue a young lady and came to take tea with her. I had been considering her seriously, only for another gentleman to enter the room and declare his intentions directly in front of me! I do not think I have ever felt more embarrassed."

Lady Harsham let out a strangled noise and Oliver, looking at her sharply, saw her waving one hand furiously in front of her face, the other hand pulling from his arm to cover her mouth. Oliver blinked in confusion, only to then realize that she was trying her best not to laugh.

"I am terribly sorry," she squeaked, her face flushing hot as she closed her eyes in clear embarrassment. "I do not mean to be laughing at your discomfort. It is only that... well, the way that you described it made me..."

Oliver began to chuckle, seeing the mirth in the situation for what was the first time since it had occurred. Seeing him laugh, Lady Harsham dissolved into giggles and Oliver began to roar with laughter, a great sense of relief and sheer pleasure beginning to wrap all around him.

And it was all because of her.

CHAPTER TEN

'*I* understand that you have a great many letters to respond to and I, who have already had a letter answered, must appear very rude indeed to be writing to you again but, all the same, I must ask for your advice.'

Jane's lips tilted upwards as she continued to read, knowing full well that this anonymous letter was from Lord Edenbridge. He had done as he had said he would and *had* written to The London Chronicle, seeking now what he ought to do since he had singled out these three young ladies.

'Should I now begin to pursue them all? Or enquire quietly about their families and characters? I have made many a mistake before, and do not wish to do so again. I understand that I may sound foolish, but it comes from a deep desire not to make any sort of mistake again.'

Jane smiled to herself as she finished the letter, only for her eyebrows to lift as she took in the postscript at the bottom.

'*If you do not wish to publish a response, I quite under-stand. However, I would be grateful for any advice you might*

*wish to give, and any notes can be sent to me at this enclosed
address.'*

She read the address quickly, recognizing that it was not
his own personal address, but one which must be his solicitor's. He still wished to keep his anonymity then, but clearly
was still hopeful of some kind of response from her. Her
heart softened with sympathy for him, recognizing that he
truly did fear that he would make some sort of foolish
mistake all over again if he did not follow advice given to
him by another.

But what can I say that would be of aid to him?

A sudden thought came to her and, with a smile on her
face, she hurried across the room and quickly began to pen a
response.

"I MUST SAY, I thought your advice to the mother seeking
what to do as regarded her eldest daughter was quite
remarkable." Lady Guilford smiled warmly as Jane ducked
her head, a little embarrassed to be offered such praise. "You
were respectful, considered, but yet careful to think on the
young lady's needs as well as her mother's."

Jane lifted her gaze, the noise of the ballroom forcing
her to speak a little louder than she might otherwise have
done.

"I am glad to hear you say that. I confess to have been a
trifle worried that I had spoken a little too firmly, whereas
what I was trying to do was to be as sympathetic as possible
– both to the mother who clearly wanted her daughter to
marry well, but also to the daughter who wished to make up
her mind as regards the gentleman in question!" She lifted
her shoulders. "I know that I should have been glad to have

been offered the chance to decide on my marriage. Lord Harsham might have appeared to be an excellent match in terms of his fortune and standing, but his character lacked any sort of kindness. Had I had the chance to know him even a little just before the betrothal was announced, I would have turned away from him directly, I am sure."

Lady Guilford nodded, her eyes searching Jane's face.

"It is because of such experiences that you are able to give such wise advice," she murmured, as Jane smiled a little sadly. "I do not know if that is much of an encouragement, but it is true, all the same."

"It is." Jane looked away, one hand pressed lightly at her stomach as a sudden swirl of nervousness ran through her. "I also received another letter from Lord Edenbridge, though I responded privately rather than sending it to be printed."

Lady Guilford's eyes widened as they stood together in the corner of the ballroom, though she said nothing.

"He has three young ladies in mind, though I do not know who they are. He is now wondering what he ought to do next."

"What he ought to do next?" Lady Guilford repeated, sounding astonished. "Surely it is just what every gentleman knows he must do – he then takes tea with them, mayhap a walk in the park, and certainly he dances with them all at balls such as this." She waved her arm in the direction of the dancers. "Why does he need advice to do that?"

Jane shrugged but tipped her head, looking out at the dancers rather than at her friend.

"I think that he is afraid. He has made some mistakes already and is all too aware of them, though he *was* able to laugh at one, which I did appreciate." Her gaze returned to Lady Guilford's. "I think that he is truly afraid that he will do something which will bring him embarrassment, and which the *ton* will take hold of thereafter." She sighed, her heart aching for him. "He appears to be such a wonderful gentleman, with a kind character and an eagerness to find the sweetest young lady to be his bride. It is only the *ton* gossiping about his lack of fortune and the mistakes that he has made already that is holding him back."

Lady Guilford leaned forward, her eyes now seeming to glow with a strange light which made Jane frown.

"Are you certain that you wish to help him?"

The frown on Jane's face dug deeper.

"Of course I am."

"Are you sure?" her friend persisted. "You appear to be thinking of him a great deal. It also seems to me as though you value his character, and think well of him. Does that not mean...?" She trailed off rather than finishing the question and Jane, not understanding in the least bit what her friend meant, kept her frown in place. Lady Guilford let out an exasperated sigh. "You have no husband, Jane. He is seeking a wife, a kind, considerate, and gentle lady – all of which you are, and more! Might you not think of approaching him yourself?"

It was as though the entire ballroom had come to a sudden stop. Jane, rooted to the spot, stared at her friend, her chest growing tighter and tighter as she fought to breathe.

"Jane." Lady Guilford put a hand to Jane's arm and suddenly, the noise of the ballroom flooded back towards her, and she took a huge breath. "I did not mean to startle you, I apologize. Might I ask if you have truly never thought about such a thing?"

Jane shook her head, her breathing coming in short, sharp gasps.

"Then I shall pretend that I said nothing of the sort," her friend continued, with a small smile. "Goodness, you have gone quite pale! Come, let us go and find a drink for you, so that you can recover a little."

"I am quite all right." Jane closed her eyes but grasped her friend's hand tightly. "It is only the thought of taking a husband again that has me so frightened."

When she opened her eyes, Lady Guilford's expression was one of pure sympathy and understanding, her eyes softening, her lips in a sad smile and her hand squeezing Jane's tightly.

"I do not want to say that I understand, for I do not, but surely you can tell that there is a great difference between Lord Harsham and Lord Edenbridge?"

Closing her eyes again and feeling a little unsteady, Jane took another breath and then blew it out, swallowing hard with it.

"Lord Harsham's true character became known to me only once we were wed," she said, her voice wobbling. "The reason my sister and her husband gave me this house and this employment is so that I would never have to think about tying myself to a gentleman again. You must understand, Louisa, that even if I thought Lord Edenbridge to be the very best of gentlemen, I do not think that I could ever bring myself to fully trust him. No, it is better for me to remain just as I am, I am sure of it."

As she spoke, a sharp pain tore through her heart and she shuddered lightly, only for Lady Guilford to embrace her, holding her tightly until the shuddering had passed.

"I am truly sorry for my foolishness," her friend said, releasing her. "I did not pause to think and, in my lack of consideration, it is clear that I have caused you great distress. I am sorry for that."

Jane swallowed but tried to smile.

"It is quite all right. I am glad that you understand now."

"I do, and I shall not make such a suggestion again, I promise you. Now, shall we go to find you something to drink all the same? You do look a little pale still."

With a nod, Jane let her friend lead her through the crowd, still feeling a little weak. It had come as something of a shock, even to herself, to see how strong her reaction had been to what her friend had suggested but, yet, all the same, Jane had to admit that her heart did hold a growing tenderness for Lord Edenbridge.

But that did not matter, she reminded herself, as a glass was pressed into her hands. She was free not to take a husband, she was *glad* she did not have to marry again, and that was all there was to consider.

I only wish that my heart did not pain itself at the thought, Jane considered, sipping the ratafia. *Lord Edenbridge needs my help, nothing more. I can only ever be a friend to him and indeed, that is all I ever want to be to him!*

That thought did not bring her any sort of happiness and, as she sipped again from the glass, Jane's heart sank low. The ballroom light seemed to dim, the music taking on a sad intonation. Sighing heavily, Jane turned to make her way back to the corner of the room, and to the shadows waiting there.

CHAPTER ELEVEN

I should not have been eavesdropping.

Oliver pushed one hand through his hair as he leaned back against the wall of the ballroom, his heart heavy. He had not meant to hear Lady Guilford and Lady Harsham's conversation, but given where they had been standing and where he had been, he had not been able to help it. He had, in fact, just been about to go and ask the lady if she would like to dance, only for Lady Guilford to ask a question which had struck Oliver sharply where he stood. Affixed to the spot on the floor, he had listened with an unwilling ear as Lady Harsham had explained in great detail why she could never consider him, and with every word that had come from her mouth, Oliver's spirits had sunk lower.

It was a strange reaction, of course, for he did not understand what it was that had done such a thing to him - for everything she had said, he both understood and accepted. After all, given what he knew of the late Lord Harsham's character, it seemed quite clear to him that the lady had been in great difficulty when it had come to her husband.

Though I do wonder what employment she was speaking of.

Shaking his head to himself, Oliver lifted his head, only to see the very person he had been thinking of coming back towards him. Her head was lowered, her steps heavy and Oliver's heart immediately squeezed with a sudden agony - though it was mostly in sympathy for what she had endured with her late husband – as well as upset over what she had said about forever being alone. That was something he did not want for her, Oliver realized, though quite why he had any sort of investment in what she did and what her future was, he could not quite say.

"Lady Harsham." Coming closer to her, Oliver smiled as her head lifted, though she did not smile back at him. "Good evening! I do hope you are well?"

"Yes, I am. Why, do not I not appear so?"

A little surprised at the slightly sharp response, Oliver shook his head.

"No, of course not. You appear just as you always are, Lady Harsham."

"Oh." Wincing, she closed her eyes and then sighed. "I apologize. I have just had a somewhat trying conversation, but that does not mean that I should be sharp in my words to you. Forgive me."

"There is nothing to forgive." He held out his arm and, much to his relief, she took it without hesitating and Oliver, letting instinct lead him, settled his other hand over hers for just a moment. "Are you quite all right?"

"Yes." She looked up at him and smiled as he took his hand away. "I am quite well. Now, tell me of these young ladies that you have considered."

"Ah." Oliver chuckled, his eyes darting around the room in the hope of spying them. "The first is Lady Henrietta, the second Miss Leverton – though I find her shy and her mother, Lady Keswick, rather overwhelming – and the third, whom I have only found this evening, is Lady Bridget."

Lady Harsham frowned.

"I do not think that I am acquainted with Miss Leverton and Lady Keswick, nor Lady Bridget though I do know Lady Henrietta."

"And what think you of her?"

The lady smiled.

"She is kind and considerate. Her manner is good and her conversation excellent. I do not think that I have heard her gossip about anyone, though that does not mean anything, she might well be inclined towards such a thing. That is something you shall have to find out for yourself, I suppose."

"Lord Dunstable has long been acquainted with their family and speaks very highly of her. I think her very pleasant, at least."

"That is good." She glanced at him. "And Lady Bridget?"

"Yes, Lady Bridget." Oliver cleared his throat, recalling the interaction that had happened only a few minutes before he had come to stand at the back of the ballroom to collect his thoughts. "I was previously acquainted with her father it seems, though I confess that I did not recall our introduction! He is the Earl of Marchfield and a very fine gentleman I think."

Lady Harsham stopped suddenly, pulling Oliver back. When he looked at her, her eyes had widened, her mouth forming a perfect circle.

A knot tied itself in his stomach.

"What is wrong?"

"Lord Marchfield?" she repeated, as Oliver nodded. "Then he must be wed to Lady Marchfield, I presume?"

"Yes," Oliver agreed, "though I do not recall being introduced to her. Why? Are you acquainted with her personally?"

At this, a hint of a smile broke out across her expression though she pulled it back very quickly indeed.

"Yes, I am afraid that I am."

"Afraid?" Oliver repeated, the knot growing tighter. "Why?"

Lady Harsham opened her mouth, closed it again, and then shook her head, frowning.

"I mayhap should not say. After all, it is not the mother that you are considering, but Lady Bridget herself! I do not want to alter your opinion of anyone, simply because their parents might be a little... difficult."

Oliver leaned a little closer to her, a sweet scent of oranges drifting towards him as he did so, making his stomach tighten all the more – though this time, for an entirely different reason.

"Please, do not hide this from me. If there is something about the lady's parents that I ought to know, then I would be grateful if you would share it."

Lady Harsham studied him.

"I do not want to take your interest from the lady, however."

"But it would not be doing so," he promised. "All it would do would encourage me to be cautious, that is all. You know that I do not want to fail yet again and therefore–"

"Very well, very well, you have convinced me!" Lady Harsham laughed softly and caught his hand for a brief moment, silencing him. "Tell me, do you recall when you came to save me from that *dire* conversation at the theatre?"

A frown tugged at Oliver's forehead.

"Yes, of course. There was a lady asking you some deeply personal and improper questions and in a manner which I thought to be very rude indeed."

Lady Harsham's lips pulled into a small, sad smile.

"That was Lady Marchfield." The knot in Oliver's stomach yanked so hard, he caught his breath in a small gasp. "I do not know what I can say of her character, for it is not all that well known to me," the lady continued, speaking a little more quickly now, as though she were doing her best to make what she had said a little sweeter. "All I know is that her words to me were a little sharp, and her conversation impolite, but that does not mean that she will always be so." Her shoulders lifted. "It might be that she is nothing short of delightful when it comes to conversing with a gentleman."

Oliver did not know how to respond. His first thought was that he had no desire to be in company with Lady Marchfield at all, and that meant forgetting about Lady Bridget entirely, only for the next thought to be of Lady Harsham herself. If he were to continue with his interest in Lady Bridget, would that not mean that his friendship with Lady Harsham would have to begin to fade? After all, he could not have her spoken to like that again, nor did he want any sort of question thrown to *him* by an improper Lady Marchfield about the lady.

"You are frowning rather heavily." Lady Harsham let out a small sigh. "Mayhap I ought not to have told you. I did not mean to react as I did, but you must know that I care about you. I care about what happens in this situation. I do not want you to be miserable and frustrated all over again!"

Oliver's eyes darted back towards her, a sudden leaping in his chest chasing away the tightness in his frame and the heaviness in his heart. Lady Harsham cared for him? Reminding himself of the conversation he had overheard, Oliver tried to dismiss it, tried to tell himself that he was being foolish and reading too much into what she had said, but that hope lingered there regardless. Lady Harsham's gaze held his, her eyes searching his as she bit her lip.

"I – I am glad that you told me."

Oliver took a deep breath and then released it, forcing a smile as he quietened the swirling emotions within his heart. He could not be foolish in this, not now. He had already heard that Lady Harsham would not take another husband, so the care she spoke of must be that of friendship, nothing more. *But why, then, did I find myself so fiercely hopeful?*

"Edenbridge?"

Oliver started lightly, realizing that he had said nothing more but had, instead, simply been staring at the lady. Clearing his throat gruffly, he shrugged and then looked away.

"I am glad you told me," he said again. "I will have to consider whether or not to continue in my pursuit of the lady. I have three that I am considering, after all, and to remove one is no bad thing."

"Though she might well be more than suitable!" Lady Harsham protested, her cheeks a little red now. "You cannot remove her from your thoughts simply because of her mother's impropriety."

"Oh, but I can," Oliver replied, chuckling at the way the lady's eyes widened. "Can you imagine what it would be like? Though you say she might well only speak in that improper manner to ladies such as yourself, I confess that I am not as convinced. Can you imagine what she would be like as a mother-in-law? There would be questions about all manner of things, questions which would make even me blush, I am sure!" Seeing Lady Harsham begin to giggle, Oliver grinned and continued, taking her hand on his arm again so that they could continue to promenade around the ballroom. "I would be asked about my estate, the investments I have made which questions, I am sure, would be in-depth and pressing for, no doubt, she would speak of my late father and his mistakes! Thereafter, there might be questions about children, about the nursemaid, the governess, the dancing master, the housekeeper, the butler... can you imagine the difficulty that would become?"

Lady Harsham was still laughing, her eyes dancing as she looked up at him.

"I suppose I can see it now," she agreed, as Oliver chuckled along with her. "Mayhap you are right."

"I believe that I am." Oliver shrugged lightly. "I have two others to consider now, I suppose. That is no bad thing."

Lady Harsham's smile faded completely, her expression now serious.

"Are you quite sure that you are glad I told you?"

Oliver nodded, reaching across again to press her hand as it sat on his arm.

"I am more than grateful," he told her, seeing that smile come again and finding his heart lighting in response. "More than you can know."

CHAPTER TWELVE

"*I* was just saying that – oh, do excuse me for a moment."

Jane smiled warmly at the two ladies who were sitting with her in the drawing room as a tap came at the door. Lady Martins and her daughter, Lady Rebecca, smiled and nodded as Jane called for the butler to enter.

"Lady Keswick and her daughter, Miss Leverton."

Jane, a little surprised, managed to keep her poise as the two ladies entered the room. She had not been introduced to either of them before, she was sure, and certainly had not been expecting a visit! Was this not one of the young ladies that Lord Edenbridge had told her he was considering? And if it was, did that have anything to do with their unexpected arrival?

"Lady Keswick, Miss Leverton." Curtseying, she smiled warmly, hiding her confusion. "How very good to meet you."

The older lady smiled, although it was a little tight, Jane considered.

"I am aware that we have not been introduced, but I do hope that you will not consider it improper."

Jane smiled.

"No, not in the least. Please, do come and join us."

"I thank you." Lady Keswick nodded to the other ladies, seemingly already acquainted with them, and then went to sit down with her daughter next to her. "I was sorry to hear of your husband's passing, Lady Harsham. I did not know him personally, but I am sure that it must have brought with it a great deal of suffering."

Jane, who considered that her marriage to Lord Harsham had been nothing but suffering, and his death, as sorrowful as it was to say, a relief from that, only smiled gently and nodded.

"You are very kind, Lady Keswick. Might I pour you some tea? It has only just been brought in."

The lady nodded though, Jane considered, Miss Leverton had not said a single word as yet. Instead, she sat quietly, her gaze resting on the floor rather than looking at Jane, her hands in her lap. Silently wondering what it was that had brought Lady Keswick and Miss Leverton to her, Jane set down the teacups and then, finally, sat down in her chair again.

Silence reigned. Jane pressed her lips together tightly, all the more confused about why Lady Keswick and Miss Leverton had come to call, and wondering why, now, there was no conversation whatsoever. Was it that Lady Keswick did not want to say anything in the company of others? Or was the silence from the simple truth that none of them were well acquainted with the other?

"Are you enjoying the Season, Miss Leverton?"

Thankfully, one of the other guests spoke, and Jane picked up her teacup to hide her sigh of relief.

Miss Leverton looked at her mother before speaking, however, almost as though she needed Lady Keswick's approval before she said a single word. Her mother gave an almost imperceptible nod and Miss Leverton then nodded.

"Yes, I am."

It was a very brief answer indeed, and Jane's eyebrows rose high in surprise. Instead of speaking a little more at length to continue with the conversation, Miss Leverton had said very little, choosing, it seemed, to bring the conversation to a close before it had even begun!

Mayhap she is shy, Jane considered, wanting to think the best of the lady. *Her mother might well be somewhat intimidating and therefore, she feels afraid of doing anything which might bring about her disapproval.*

"Tell me, Miss Leverton, do you enjoy dancing?" Letting a light lilt lift her voice, Jane kept her expression warm in the hope of encouraging the young lady. "Have you danced many dances?"

Before Miss Leverton could speak, however, Lady Keswick set her cup down, cleared her throat, and then pinned Jane with a sharp gaze – sharper than Jane had expected.

"I shall get directly to the point." She shot a hard look towards Lady Martins and her daughter. "I know that you will not speak of this to anyone, Lady Martins, for if there is any sort of gossip about my daughter and what I am about to say now, then I will know who to blame."

Jane blinked in surprise, seeing now just how forthright and intimidating Lady Keswick could be. Lady Martins seemed to shrink back in her chair, her words mumbled as she promised not to say anything to anyone about what was to be spoken.

"Good." Lady Keswick returned her gaze to Jane and

Jane shuddered lightly. "You appear to be well acquainted with Lord Edenbridge. He has come to speak with my daughter on a few occasions and has danced with her twice, though I was not particularly pleased with her response." Sniffing, she sent a hard look towards Miss Leverton, who did not respond. "It was not as encouraging as it might have been."

Still a little taken aback by how quickly the subject had changed – and to the subject it had changed *to*, Jane spread out her hands.

"What is it that I can do in this, Lady Martins? It seems to me as though this is a matter between your daughter and Lord Edenbridge."

"Except that, as I have said, *you* are well acquainted with Lord Edenbridge, I think. I have seen you walking with him, laughing with him, and dancing with him. Tell me, are you interested in a connection with him? Or is there a connection already there?"

Heat poured into Jane's chest, racing upwards into her cheeks, even her hands growing hot and clammy as she understood the lady's meaning.

"That is a somewhat inappropriate question, Lady Keswick."

The lady only shrugged.

"I care not. What I do care about is my daughter. I should like to know whether or not there is a closeness between yourself and Lord Edenbridge that might otherwise prevent him from pulling himself wholeheartedly towards my daughter, should he desire to do so."

Jane, wishing that there were no other guests present, lifted her chin.

"I think it is disappointing to know that a widow, such as myself, cannot even walk with a gentleman and dance with him without there coming some suggestion of impropriety. In answer to your question, no, I am only friends with Lord Edenbridge, and am glad to be so."

Lady Keswick said nothing for a few moments, searching Jane's face as though she thought her to be telling untruths. Jane remained exactly where she was, her hands now clasped in her lap as she waited for Lady Keswick's response. She had to pray that Lady Martins and her daughter would do exactly what they had promised, and not breathe a word of this conversation to anyone, for what rumors would be spread through London otherwise! That was not at all what she wanted – and it was the very last thing that Lord Edenbridge needed!

"If that is so, then I am glad to hear it. Though I must ask, Lady Harsham, what is the state of his fortune? I have heard that his father was practically impoverished before he died and that the new Lord Edenbridge was left with barely two coins to rub together!"

"I cannot speak to that," Jane answered, calmly, "for I do not have such a long acquaintance with Lord Edenbridge to say what it is that might or might not have been, as regarded his father. However, I do know that he is certainly not impoverished! He has spoken of it to me, about the difficulties that he faced and the trials which have come with it for, even though his fortune has greatly improved since he took on the title, the *ton* appears to refuse to believe it. That is a great shame, I must say, for he is a gentleman of excellent character and standing."

A light came into Lady Keswick's eyes and, for some inexplicable reason, Jane found her spirits sinking very low indeed. Surely it could not be because she was defending Lord Edenbridge to Lady Keswick, she considered, for she was glad to do so. She did not want the *ton* to think him poor and lacking when he was not, and she was quite certain that he deserved a good deal more than he was given by way of respect and consideration – so why, now, did she find herself feeling dispirited by the conversation?

"That is good to know. I would, of course, require proof of such a thing if his attentions towards my daughter increase." She smiled and settled back in her chair a little, as though all that Jane had said had satisfied her completely. "Did you know that he has asked to take tea with her? Does that not speak well of things? I know that she is very quiet and somewhat shy, but that does not seem to trouble Lord Edenbridge!"

"No, I am sure it would not," Jane murmured, noticing the flush that came into Miss Leverton's cheeks. She felt a little sorrowful for the young lady, for her mother was speaking of her as though she was not even present, and that could not bring her any sort of happiness. "I am sure that – oh."

Hearing a tap at the door again and silently hoping that this was another guest so that she might alter the conversation entirely, Jane called.

The door opened and with seeming reluctance, the butler came in rather slowly. About to berate him, Jane's eyes widened in astonishment as she took in what he held in his hand – a silver tray with a good many letters spread out neatly upon it.

The London Chronicle!

Her anxiety began to swirl and quickly, Jane rose to her feet and came towards him quickly, gathering up the letters in her hands.

"Forgive me, my Lady, but you did ask for these to be brought to you as soon as possible," the butler murmured, so that only she could hear. "I was not certain whether I should do so given that you have company but–"

"It is quite all right." With a nod, Jane dismissed him and then turned back to her guests, all of whom were now staring at the great many letters that she had in her hands. "You must forgive the interruption, I beg of you," she said, a sudden fright running through her as she saw the questions burning in every expression. "I expect to receive a good deal of correspondence this week and the butler knows how eager I am to receive the letters."

"That is certainly a good deal of correspondence, I must say." Lady Keswick tilted her head and looked steadily at the letters, as if she were trying to count them to ascertain just how many Jane held. "Goodness, I am surprised that you have received so many in one afternoon! You must be very popular indeed."

Jane swallowed and then set the stacked letters on a small table at the side of the room which gave her just a few minutes to compose herself. Pasting a light smile on her face, she let out a bright laugh as she turned back to her guests, spreading out her hands.

"I do not think that it is because I am popular, Lady Keswick, but more than I have a good many acquaintances who wish to hear all about the delights of London. I write as much as I can, and as often as I can but sometimes, I do feel as though even that is not enough!"

"Yes, I can imagine." Lady Martins rose to her feet, her daughter beside her. "To those who have never been to London, your letters must be quite thrilling!"

"That is kind of you to say," Jane answered, desperately hoping that Lady Keswick would accept this explanation without further questions. "I suppose that is true, though I do not ever think of myself and my letters in such terms!"

Lady Keswick sniffed.

"I suppose that is because you have not been in society for all that long, Lady Harsham. There cannot be too much to say as yet, can there?"

Jane kept her smile fixed.

"There is enough to make them all very excited indeed," she said, a little upset that the lie came so easily to her though, at the same time, she did not want to emphasize it further. "My sister's letter will be here too, I am sure. She is a little anxious for me, though I do keep reminding her that she has no need to be."

This seemed to make Lady Keswick soften just a little, for her lips curved and she nodded.

"That is understandable. She must have been very worried about you and your future when your husband passed away. Now, however, you have a chance to find yourself another match, if you so wish." She tilted her head, studying Jane with a sharpened eye. "Is that why you are in London?"

Utterly astonished at Lady Keswick's question, Jane stared at her, wide-eyed, for a few minutes, silence flooding the room. Miss Leverton dropped her head, her chin practically on her chest, her eyes closed as though embarrassed, but Lady Martins and *her* daughter both quietly took their seats again. Jane did not know whether it was because they truly wished to hear what she would say, or because they did not know what to do, but either way, she was not about to satisfy Lady Keswick's question with an answer.

"Given that we are not well acquainted, Lady Keswick, I am afraid that I have no intention of sharing any of my personal thoughts and considerations as regards the Season and my future." Her voice rang with a firmness that seemed to surprise Lady Keswick, given the way that her eyebrows leaped up, but Jane was not yet finished with her response. "I might also say, Lady Keswick, that I find your manner a little rude," Jane continued, choosing to be quite frank in how she spoke. "As you said yourself, we are not acquainted, though I have been glad to welcome you into my home. Thereafter, you have not only questioned me about my connection to Lord Edenbridge, suggesting that there might be more to our friendship than there appears, and thereafter, asking me whether I am seeking a match this Season or not! I do not take pleasure in such questions and must hope that, should our connection continue, there will be less of what I have experienced this afternoon."

Lady Keswick blinked and then looked at her daughter sharply. Jane saw Miss Leverton's lips moving, though she could not make out what was said. Thereafter, Lady Keswick forced a smile and then returned her gaze to Jane, though there was nothing but shadows in her expression now.

"I must ask for your forgiveness. You understand, I am sure, that I asked only about Lord Edenbridge for the sake of my daughter? The latter questions, I confess, came simply from my own curiosity, though that is no excuse." She rose to her feet, Miss Leverton beside her, and Lady Martins quickly followed suit. "Do forgive my lack of propriety. I can assure you, it will not happen again. Thank you again for your welcome and the tea. It was all most enjoyable."

Jane offered the lady a small smile but did not feel it within her heart. She did not much like Lady Keswick she decided, for to speak so bluntly, and with such inconsideration, did not speak well of her character.

"Thank you." Lady Martins bobbed a quick curtsey and

Jane's smile grew wider and a good deal more genuine. "We did enjoy our conversation very much."

"I am glad."

Jane inclined her head and then watched as all four ladies left the room, leaving her to stand alone.

The relief which washed over her was palpable. The moment that the door shut, Jane sank back down into her chair and looked over towards the stack of letters. Her advice was becoming a rather popular feature in The London Chronicle, but to receive ten letters within the space of a single day was rather overwhelming! She would have to read every one, and then decide which would be the best one or two or even three to reply to. The rest would either have to be set aside for the following day, or discarded completely, which Jane did not want to do.

"No doubt more letters will come tomorrow," she murmured to herself, wandering over to the small stack of letters on the table. Her heart began to grow heavier as she thought about what answers she might give, what sunshine she might be able to bring to an otherwise darkened situation.

But then it lifted.

Has Lord Edenbridge written to me?

The thought stirred her heart and within moments, Jane was rifling through the letters, trying to ascertain which, if any, had been sent by him.

And then, she found it.

Recognizable simply by the way he wrote his letters, Jane's heart leaped as she took it out from amongst the others, only to then frown, hard.

Why am I so delighted to have found his letter to me?

Blinking, she looked down at the letter again, trying to make the joy in her heart fade simply by sheer determination, but it would not. Instead, it only grew and grew and grew as her fingers itched to break the seal and open up the letter, to read the words that he had written to her, and to ascertain what it was that he sought help for next.

Jane swallowed hard and then set the letter down abruptly, blinking furiously as she tried to calm and quieten her emotions.

Instead, they only grew louder in the face of her defiance.

CHAPTER THIRTEEN

The hope of a response to his letter was so great that Oliver felt almost feverish as he paced up and down his drawing room. In the last sennight, he had taken tea with Lady Keswick and her daughter, Miss Leverton, and now he had just returned from a second walk with Lady Henrietta, though her mother had walked *with* them, not even so much as a little behind, as he had hoped that she might. Lady Henrietta had been very pleasing in her conversation, and when she had smiled at him there had been warmth there which had also pleased him greatly. They had not spoken of his fortune, of his supposed *lack* of fortune, at least, and what he had said in that regard had been that he was well-settled and quite contented. This was spoken in the hope that she would understand his meaning, and not believe any rumors of his being impoverished. Likewise, Lady Keswick and her daughter had not asked him anything specific regarding his situation and standing, and though Miss Leverton had smiled and spoken to him in conversation about various other things, she had not been as warm in her manner as Lady Henrietta. That being said, he did find Miss Leverton a little prettier than Lady Henrietta and thus, he now found himself in something of a bind. What was he now to do? Both ladies pleased him, and he appeared to be pleasing to them and thus, their connection could continue – but in what way? Ought he to continue to encourage both connections at the same time, knowing that only one could lead to courtship? Or ought he to decide now which one he would pursue a little more strenuously, in the hope that all would go right? A little uncertain, he had written again to The London Chronicle, sure that he would be given some excellent advice on how to proceed.

Idly, Oliver began to wonder about who the writer was. To his mind, he had no doubt that it was a lady, for the advice given was always so very considered and, he thought, rang with the voice of a gentle but astute lady who knew society well enough to speak of it with great understanding. A lady of the *ton*, then? But someone who, mayhap, required that employment – for, surely, it would be a paid position, not something that one would do voluntarily.

"Though," he murmured, still pacing up and down the room, "I must wonder if they are determined to keep their name a secret there, for fear that someone will discover her identity and then tell all of society about it! Is that the reason that the writer remains anonymous?"

A knock came at the door and Oliver practically cried out his encouragement to enter, only for none other than Lord Dunstable to walk through the door, a somewhat bemused expression on his face.

"My friend." He lifted an eyebrow. "Are you quite all right? You look to be a little... well, I do not know what it is, but there is something about your expression that seems a little unusual."

Oliver waved him in.

"Brandy?" Seeing his friend nod, he went to pour two measures. "I am waiting for a letter from The London Chronicle. I write too many to be responded to in the newspaper itself, you understand, though I believe that the letter-writer has taken pity on me, for the last reply I received was sent to my solicitors, just as I had requested. I am waiting now for my solicitor's man to bring me another reply from the lady, should there be one."

"The lady?" Lord Dunstable looked surprised. "How do you know–"

"Oh, I do not know for certain. I am only surmising. However, I wrote to ask what I must do next, for Lady Henrietta and Miss Leverton are both still in my consideration! Neither has asked me about my fortune, both seem quite content to be in my company. Our conversation was good – though Lady Henrietta's was better – and I find them both quite lovely, though I confess to being drawn to Miss Leverton a little more in that regard."

Lord Dunstable chuckled, swirling the brandy in his glass.

"I am glad to hear you say that you have not one, but *two* ladies whom you are considering," he said, now grinning ear to ear. "This is a vast change from the last time we spoke at length about such things!"

Oliver laughed.

"Yes, it is, I suppose!"

Another knock came at the door and Oliver called out again quickly, ignoring the way that his friend laughed at him. The butler came in with a letter, just as Oliver had hoped, though behind him then came another guest, someone that Oliver had not expected to see.

"Lady Harsham." Blinking, Oliver set the letter behind his back and bowed. "Good afternoon."

"I am sorry to call on you without warning," she said, smiling a greeting to Lord Dunstable. "I need not stay if you have guests. I do not want to intrude, not in the least bit."

Oliver spread out one hand towards an empty chair.

"Please, do sit down and join us," he said as Lord Dunstable nodded. "We were not speaking of anything severe, I assure you, and we would be glad to have your company." This was spoken with as much warmth as he could put into his voice, and he found that it was true, what he had just said. He *was* glad to have her with him, was delighted to see her in his townhouse, in fact. His heart seemed to have lifted, his smile was brighter, and he could not remove it from his face, not even if he tried. "Can I call for a tea tray?"

She shook her head.

"I will not stay long."

"Please." Oliver smiled as brightly as he could. "We would be glad of your company, I am sure. Please, stay if you would like and I can ring for the tea tray now. Look," he continued, lifting the letter up, "I am sure that I have another reply from The London Chronicle, for this is my solicitor's writing. Do you not want to know what is within it?"

This made Lady Harsham laugh, and she spread out her hands.

"I think that you have convinced me, though you do not need to tell me about the letter, if you do not wish to. I understand that you may wish to keep it to yourself."

Oliver laughed and shook his head, going to ring the bell before breaking open the seal.

"Not in the least! Both you and Lord Dunstable are aware of my ongoing conversation with The London Chronicle, and I have no desire to hide it from you."

Unfolding the letter, he paused as the room fell silent while he read the few lines. Then, he looked up. "You see?" Grinning now, he waved the letter around as though Lord Dunstable and Lady Harsham would somehow be able to distinguish what was written there. "There is wonderful advice given here, just precisely what I needed to hear!"

"And what were you asking?" Lord Dunstable wanted to know, though Lady Harsham remained silent, no doubt too polite to ask. "What help did you seek?"

"It is about the two young ladies I have been pursuing," Oliver explained, quickly. "Lady Henrietta is one and Miss Leverton the other. I find them both interesting, albeit in different ways and, given that neither of them has asked me about my fortune – or lack thereof – I have been uncertain as to what I ought to do next."

Lady Harsham's lips twitched.

"Then you have found the advice helpful, yes? You now know what you must do?"

Oliver nodded, still brandishing the letter.

"Yes, I do. I am to talk openly about my fortune and my struggles to each of them so that they fully understand my situation. I shall see their reaction and the reaction of their father or mother. That will help me a good deal."

"And if both are as understanding as can be?" Lord Dunstable asked, a small smile on his lips. "What then?"

"Then I shall have to make a decision as to which lady I am drawn to more," Oliver replied, thinking that the last few lines of the letter were most encouraging. "She – the lady who writes, for I am sure it is a lady – states that I am clearly in earnest and that my heart is very tender indeed. She suggests that I must make certain that whichever lady I choose is worthy of that, though I find myself a little flattered by that."

Lord Dunstable shrugged, though Lady Harsham's expression softened.

"I think I quite agree," she said, so quietly that Oliver barely heard it. When his eyes met hers, Lady Harsham's widened, as though she had not intended him to hear her speak so. She licked her lips and then smiled, though it did not hold the same gentleness as before. "In speaking of these things, I should tell you that the reason for my calling upon you is... well, I do not want to gossip, but I wanted to speak openly with you about my recent visit from Lady Keswick and her daughter."

Oliver stood up straight, shock ringing through him.

"They came to speak with you?"

Lady Harsham nodded, a tiny smile at the edge of her mouth.

"Yes, they did, even though we have never been introduced!"

"That is a little unusual." Oliver glanced at Lord Dunstable, but his eyes were on Lady Harsham. "Was there a purpose in their visit?"

Lady Harsham's eyes twinkled.

"Oh yes, they wanted to speak to me about you."

Oliver blinked rapidly, a cold hand settling over his heart for just a moment before the sensation dissipated.

"You know that I spoke well of you, I am sure," she continued, perhaps seeing his surprise. "It is not as though I would have said anything cruel or untrue."

"Did... did they speak to you about my fortune?"

Lady Harsham nodded.

"They did, but I made certain to inform them of what I knew, though I did say that I knew very little. However, I reassured the ladies that you were not about to sell your estate to regain any funds and that you were, in fact, a good deal better situated than you had been when you first took on the title."

A long breath escaped Oliver's lips.

"I thank you."

"They also..." Lady Harsham's voice dropped, and she shook her head, her eyes squeezing closed for a moment. "It is embarrassing for me to even speak of, and I confess that I was utterly astonished to hear this from a lady whom I was not even well acquainted with, but they did ask if there was any sort of connection between you and I." Scarlet ran through her cheeks, but her eyes opened, and she looked at him directly. "Thereafter, she even went on to ask me about my intentions for the Season, which I found to be utterly astonishing!"

"Goodness." Oliver rubbed one hand over his face, finding that his own face was hot. "I am sorry that you had to endure such impertinence. I thought that you had already dealt with such things quite enough, only for Lady Keswick to offer you more!"

Much to his relief, however, Lady Harsham did not seem in the least bit upset. Instead, she only shrugged and smiled, shooting a bright look towards Lord Dunstable as the tea tray was finally brought in.

"I am sure that she is only being as careful as she can for the sake of her daughter," she answered, a little more quietly than before. "The other situation was solely because that lady is who she is in her character. When it comes to Lady Keswick, I am quite certain that it came from a good intention, though spoken poorly."

Understanding what she meant – and seeing that she did not want to mention Lady Marchfield in front of Lord Dunstable – Oliver nodded.

"I understand."

"This is Miss Leverton's mother, yes?" Lord Dunstable ran one hand over his chin, his eyes thoughtful as Oliver nodded again. "I must say, I do think that Miss Leverton is a very quiet creature indeed! I have tried to speak to her before and she barely said a word or two back to me – and even to do that, she seemed to have to make certain that her mother had given her approval to speak!"

"Yes, I know what you mean," Oliver agreed, as Lady Harsham nodded her understanding. "She did speak a little more to me, but the conversation lacked any sort of warmth." He shook his head. "Would that I could be in private conversation with her! Then I might be able to ascertain as to whether or not she is truly a very reserved young lady, or if that quietness comes from her mother's somewhat overbearing presence."

Lady Harsham smiled, though Oliver did not see any light in her eyes, however.

"I am sure that I could assist you in that regard. Why do you not try to speak with the lady while I engage her mother in conversation? Would that not help?"

"It might." Oliver shrugged. "Though whether I will need to actually remove her from her mother's presence before she will talk freely, who can say?"

"It would be worth trying," Lord Dunstable agreed, "though I have also had a thought. Why do I not hold a masquerade ball?"

Oliver's heart leaped with a sudden thrill.

"A capital idea! Would that I had thought of it first!"

Lord Dunstable grinned.

"Then by all means, why do *you* not host the masquerade ball instead?"

Taking no offense at this, Oliver beamed at his friend, nodding fervently.

"I should be glad to!"

"And I would be more than willing to assist you, where necessary," Lady Harsham said, making Oliver's heart lift all the more. "And I can inform you as to who Miss Leverton is, if you wish? We ladies have a much easier time identifying one another under the masks than most gentlemen seem to do!"

She giggled as she said this, and Oliver's heart warmed, delight filling him. He took her in for another moment, seeing the way that her eyes danced, the brightness there and the joy in her expression – and realized that she was beautiful.

"Edenbridge?"

Looking at Lord Dunstable, Oliver cleared his throat, embarrassed to have been caught staring at Lady Harsham.

"Forgive me, I was lost in thought about the masquerade ball. Yes, Lady Harsham, that would be very helpful."

"And you will invite Lady Henrietta too?"

Oliver nodded, another idea coming to him.

"And," he continued, a little more quietly, "I might also invite the writer of The London Chronicle."

For a long moment, no one responded. Lord Dunstable looked interested in the notion, but Lady Harsham's face had gone a little pale, her lips thin and her eyes wide.

"You do not think it a good idea?" Directing the question at her, Oliver lifted both his shoulders. "I have been wondering who she is. I would simply invite her so that she might not only keep her identity secret, should she wish it, but also as an expression of thanks for what she has done for me thus far."

Lady Harsham blinked and then looked away.

"I think, Lord Edenbridge, that your thought of consideration is a very good one," she answered, though her words came slowly. "I suppose I might be concerned that your intention would be for her to reveal herself to you in that regard. And I must assume that someone in the writer's position would be most intent upon keeping their anonymity in place!"

A tiny smile flickered across Oliver's face.

"I cannot pretend that there is not a part of me that would like to know the truth, yes, but my intention is not to do such a thing. It would be meant only as gratitude."

Lady Harsham considered this and then nodded though she did not quite meet his gaze.

"Then I can see no reason for you not to write to the lady," she replied, though there was still an expression of concern on her face. "Whether she will accept or not, however, is an entirely different matter."

"I do hope she does," Oliver answered, as Lady Harsham reached for her teacup. "For I should very much like to offer her my thanks, whether in person or otherwise. I do not think that I would be where I am at present without her advice – I might well be back at my estate, lost in gloom and suffering the doldrums!"

This made laughter break out in the room and Oliver grinned, glad that the mood had lightened. A fluttering excitement grew in his chest, however, as he thought of the masquerade ball. Yes, he would have the chance to speak to Miss Leverton alone, but would he not also have the opportunity to get to know the real letter writer from The London Chronicle? Oliver had to admit to a growing curiosity about her identity, though he was truly grateful for the advice she had given him thus far, no matter who she was. He smiled softly to himself at the thought of meeting her, though quite how he would recognize her at a masquerade ball, he did not know! Somehow, in some way, Oliver considered, he would make certain that she knew just how thankful he was for all that she had done for him, and for the happiness which, he prayed, he might soon find.

CHAPTER FOURTEEN

*S*miling as she took Lord Edenbridge's arm, Jane did all that she could to smother the feelings that were trying to expand in her heart as he smiled at her. Ever since he had spoken of the soon-to-occur masquerade ball, and his hope of inviting the lady who wrote in The London Chronicle, she had found her heart doing all manner of strange things, rendering her nothing short of lost in confusion. Why she should feel anything for the gentleman, aside from friendship, she could not say, for there was certainly nothing else that ought to be present within her, surely?

"You do not look as though you are enjoying the evening, Lady Harsham."

Jane looked up at him.

"No?"

"No." With a slight lift of his eyebrow and a quirk of his lips – both of which sent a sparkling light into his brown eyes, he lifted his shoulders. "Might you wish to dance?"

"To dance?" she repeated, a streak of what felt like anticipation rising up within her, though she set that aside quickly. "Goodness, I do not think that I have danced the waltz in some time!"

That streak quickly turned into heat which wrapped itself around her, before then dissipating into a chill as Lord Edenbridge chuckled. It was not because of his laughter that she shivered, but because the thought of being in his arms, of being so close to him, almost terrified her.

But why?

"That does not mean that you have forgotten the steps, I am sure," he told her, with such a sweet encouragement in his voice that Jane did not think that she could refuse, not without appearing rude or giving the impression that she simply did not want to dance with him! "What say you?"

Jane took a deep breath but forced a smile.

"Yes, of course. I would be glad to."

"Capital!" He sounded so happy that she had accepted that Jane could not help but quieten her anxiety, feeling herself relaxing just a little as she looked up at him. "I am already looking forward to it."

"Are you sure that you do not want to dance the waltz with either Miss Leverton or Lady Henrietta?" she ventured, reminding herself that he was already pursuing two young ladies and saw her only as a friend and nothing more. "I am sure that both of them would be glad to step out with you."

Lord Edenbridge shook his head.

"I am afraid that Miss Leverton has no permission to dance the waltz and Lady Henrietta's waltz has been taken by another."

Jane looked up at him again, expecting him to sound disappointed but, much to her surprise, he did not. Instead, he was smiling down at her as though he was pleased that *she* would be dancing with him instead of one of them.

Her heart leaped, and Jane turned her gaze away.

"Ah, I can see Lady Guilford." Jane glanced up at him again but did not look him in the eyes, her whole being seeming to writhe with a mixture of uncertainty and fear that swept over her completely. "Might you excuse me for a few minutes, Lord Edenbridge?"

With an easy smile, he nodded.

"But of course. I will come and find you again in time for the waltz."

It was with a sense of urgency that Jane hurried towards Lady Guilford, though she could not explain why. Seeing her friend glance towards her – and then for her smile to fade – Jane caught her arm and, her heart pounding in a way that she had never expected, quietly begged her to walk with her for a short while around the ballroom.

"But of course." Lady Guilford smiled at the others she had been speaking with, excused herself, and then fell into step with Jane, bending her head close to hers. "My dear friend, whatever is the matter? You have gone as pale as can be! Are you unwell?"

"I – I do not know." Jane closed her eyes briefly, a breath shuddering out of her. "Louisa, whatever has come over me? Lord Edenbridge asked me to dance, and I felt myself glad to be asked, only for my whole being to suddenly turn weak with fear!"

Lady Guilford stopped walking and turned to look into Jane's eyes, though Jane closed hers again, trying to regain a sense of composure.

"He asked you to dance?"

"The waltz," Jane answered, opening her eyes and looking back at her friend, her voice barely louder than a whisper. "The closest, the most intimate of dances. Why do

I suddenly fear it, Louisa? Why do I now fear being close to *him?*"

A small, soft smile began to spread across Lady Guilford's face as Jane pressed her lips tight together, steadying herself.

"My dear friend, could it be that what you denied so vehemently before might, in fact, be true?"

"Denied?"

"Yes, your denial that there might be something more than just friendship between yourself and Lord Edenbridge," Lady Guilford said, gently. "I spoke to you because I believed that there *might* be something, but you refused to even consider the idea, I think."

Jane nodded.

"That is because I was sure... no, Louisa. I *cannot* let myself be drawn into this!"

"No?" Her friend tipped her head just a little. "And why would that be?"

Trying to answer, Jane opened her mouth and then closed it again, unable to give any sort of explanation for why she felt this way. It was as if part of her could see what was being offered, but the fear that was within her over it was so great that she could not... *would* not... let herself consider it.

"You are afraid." It was not a question but a clear statement and Jane, recognizing that there was no need for her to pretend otherwise, nodded. "But why are you afraid?" Lady Guilford pressed, still speaking gently, though her questions felt like sharp knives pressing into Jane's skin. "You know that Lord Edenbridge is a good man. There is nothing that he has said or done to frighten you, is there?" Jane shook her head, wordlessly. "He is nothing like Lord Harsham," Lady Guilford continued, as tears quickly sprang into Jane's eyes at the mention of her late husband. "I can see that, and I am certain that you can too."

"But what if he hides a good deal of his character, just as Lord Harsham did?" Words began to tumble from Jane's mouth, her heart pounding as she gazed at her friend, her vision a little blurred. "Lord Harsham hid his cruelty from most of the *ton*, though I will admit that some knew of his true character. What if Lord Edenbridge is the same?"

Sympathy poured into Lady Guilford's expression.

"Oh, my dear friend." She came closer and took both of Jane's hands in her own. "You are afraid that, should you let yourself be a little more vulnerable when it comes to Lord Edenbridge, he will then turn into a gentleman you do not recognize? That there is a part of him – a big part of him – that he is hiding from you?" She shook her head as Jane tried to swallow past the knot in her throat, feeling pain clasp at her heart. "That is an injury that your late husband placed upon your heart," Lady Guilford continued, gently, "and it has clearly not yet healed. I can understand why you would be afraid, but you must understand that there are very few gentlemen like your late husband. Most of them are just as they seem! I say this with confidence, for I know my own husband is one such gentleman, and all of his closest friends are of similar ilk. You need not fear that Lord Edenbridge will be like Lord Harsham, Jane! You will rob yourself of any potential happiness that might come from being honest with your own heart and, mayhap, with him!"

Tears began to burn in Jane's eyes as she fought to speak. She could not find any words to explain all that was building in her chest. She understood what her friend was saying, and wanted to believe it, wanted to take it in, but there was too much fear there, too much dread over what might be, should she be honest about her heart, as Lady Guilford had suggested.

"You *must* trust him!" Lady Guilford said, her fingers tightening on Jane's, her eyes searching hers. "Tell him of your fear, if you wish!"

"Tell him?" Jane croaked, pulling back from the idea immediately. "I do not think that I can! I would not be able to do such a thing!"

"Why not?" The thought of speaking to Lord Edenbridge of her late husband and all of his cruelty sent a tremor through her. "Do you not think he would understand?" Lady Guilford asked, softly.

"He would wonder why I was telling him!" Jane exclaimed, pulling her hands out of Lady Guilford's. "He would ask why–"

"Of course he would," her friend interrupted, gently, "but then, mayhap, you could share with him the truth." Smiling as Jane shook her head, Lady Guilford shrugged lightly. "I think that you would be very happy with Lord Edenbridge, Jane. You are close in your acquaintance with him, he seems very happy to be in your company, and you seem glad to be in his – and that is what I want for you. I *want* you to be happy."

Jane swallowed and then looked away.

"I *am* happy." Her voice rasped, betraying her emotion, for no sense of genuine happiness spread into her words. "I am. Truly."

"Are you?" Lady Guilford's quiet question made Jane's skin prickle, and she looked back at her, seeing how her friend's eyebrow lifted, a glimmer of a smile still on her lips. "Then if you are so happy and contented, tell me how you will truly feel when Lord Edenbridge decides to take a bride? When he chooses one of the two ladies he is considering?"

Thinking of this, Jane tried to pretend that she would be more than contented, tilting her chin up so that she could speak with confidence... but nothing more than sadness hit her. Her shoulders rounded, her heart dropped to the floor and her spirit grew heavy.

She closed her eyes.

"I know that you have the town house and your employment, and I understand that you are afraid of what might be, should you listen to all that your heart is saying." Lady Guilford embraced Jane for a moment, then released her, her hands at her shoulders, her gaze fixed and determined. "But you must consider what you will lose if you do *not* tell him. That is all I am saying to you."

Jane nodded but shivered, the thought of being honest and open with Lord Edenbridge in that way making her tremble with dread. She feared that, in doing so, he might then reveal the truth of his character, just as Lord Harsham had done the day of their wedding.

"I have come to find you, as I have said!" Lord Edenbridge appeared just as Jane shivered, yet again, making the smile on his face fade away. "Are you quite all right?"

Jane nodded.

"I am." Pushing down everything within her heart and mind so that she barely felt or thought of anything other than what was now expected of her, she accepted his arm. "Thank you."

"You are certain that you are quite ready to dance? We do not have to, if you do not wish to."

The concern in his voice made Jane's heart squeeze and, despite her attempts at pushing everything away, she could not help but let warmth flood through her as she nodded.

"I think a waltz would be a capital idea," Lady Guilford remarked, sending a kind smile towards Jane, who could not respond in any other way but with a small smile of her own. "I think I shall go in search of my husband and demand that we dance also!"

This made Jane laugh and, with that sweetness beginning to fill her heart, she was led to the dance floor by Lord Edenbridge and, after a moment, stepped into his arms.

It was as though the entire world shifted as she danced. The ground seemed to move under her feet, weakness beginning to take hold, forcing her to tighten her grip on his hand and shoulder. Lord Edenbridge did not remark on this, however, though his eyes searched hers, the worry within them offering her a sense of comfort which she grasped hold of.

Strength slowly began to return to her as the waltz continued. She did not know where it had come from, but the weakness in her limbs began to flee, her poise returning as her gaze melded with his. There was a slow growing happiness in her now, something that sent out heat into the very tips of her fingers, seeming to push back the fear that she had felt so strongly only moments ago.

And then, Lord Edenbridge smiled.

Jane's heart exploded. She could not quite understand it, her breath hitching, her chest tight as she lost herself in his eyes. There was something so wonderful about this moment, as though she had found something that, for a long time, she had been searching for and had been unable to discover. Lord Edenbridge pulled her just a little closer, as though he knew all that she was feeling and wanted it to linger, and Jane's heart burned hot again.

Dare I confess to him what I have only just begun to realize myself?

She pressed her lips together, realizing that she had been dancing with him without even thinking of the steps, that they had been moving as one across the dance floor. Lady Guilford had recognized that there was a closeness between them, an intimacy that was continually growing and, as the dance slowly came to an end, Jane realized just how much she did not want to step away from him. Instead of the dread she had felt in stepping out to dance, she now wanted to linger a little longer, to have his arm at her waist, to have her hand in his.

"I think you are a wonderful dancer, Lady Harsham."

"Jane."

The word came from her before she could even have thought to keep it back, seeing the way his eyebrows shot towards his hairline.

"I do not like being continually reminded of my husband," she said, as the other couples began to leave the dance floor. "We are closely enough acquainted for me to ask you to call me Jane whenever you can, though I understand that in a place such as this, it would not be right, given what rumors might spring up if someone should overhear you."

Lord Edenbridge considered this for a moment, then nodded, turning so he could accompany her back to the side of the ballroom where the other guests stood. Jane's hand went to his arm almost without her thinking, though he did not seem in the least bit upset at this.

"I do hope I have not embarrassed you in any way by speaking so. There is no need for you to do as I ask." Heat seared her cheeks as she looked away, but Lord Edenbridge stopped suddenly, just as they reached the other guests and Jane turned to look up at him.

"You must not apologize," he said, with such a softness

in his voice that the heat in Jane's face grew all the more. "I am honored, truly, that you would not only ask me such a thing, but that you would be so vulnerable with me as regards your late husband." His eyes searched hers. "I would never speak a word of whatever you chose to share with me. I pray that you know that."

Jane swallowed and looked away from him, suddenly unable to look into his face.

"I do," she said, a little huskily. "Given all that you have endured from the *ton,* I am certain that you would never share a word of what I have said to you."

Lord Edenbridge caught her hand and then, before she could even take a breath, pressed a kiss to the back of her hand.

"I am grateful for the trust you have in me, Jane," he said, using her name for the first time. "I swear to you, I shall never make you regret it."

Try as she might, Jane could not say a single word in response, given the tumbling, swirling, astonishing feelings that poured through her. All she could do was smile and wonder, desperately, whatever she was to do with all that she now felt.

CHAPTER FIFTEEN

"*L*ady Henrietta, thank you for walking with me again." Oliver smiled as he lifted his head from his bow, offering the lady his arm. "It seems to me that you are very fond of Hyde Park. Is this not the second time that you have requested that we take a walk here?"

Lady Henrietta glanced at him.

"Yes, it is."

Her lips did not curve into a smile, however, and her eyes were a little watchful, as though she expected him to berate her because of such a request, and Oliver was quick to encourage her.

"I do like Hyde Park very much," he continued, wondering why she was not smiling. Was it, mayhap, because her mother insisted on remaining close to them? "I think that there will be many fine acquaintances whom we may meet this afternoon."

Again, Lady Henrietta glanced at him, only to look away.

"Yes, I am sure that there will be."

"I – I wonder if..." Recalling the advice given to him by

the writer of The London Chronicle, Oliver cleared his throat. "I did wonder if we might speak of my supposed lack of fortune, Lady Henrietta?" This brought her eyes snapping back to his. "I know that there are many rumors about me and my present standing," Oliver continued with a small smile, though inwardly, he felt his stomach knotting. "I should like to speak to you about that, if you would permit me?"

"Of course."

Oliver frowned. There did not appear to be any real interest in the lady's voice but, then again, he considered, it was not right for a young lady such as herself to show real interest in that way. They were not meant to show any concern over matters such as inheritance and fortune and therefore, no doubt, she wanted him to think her quite proper.

"My father, when he passed away, did not leave the estates in a good state," he said clearly, choosing to be entirely honest rather than hide the truth. "The estate was in need of repair in some parts, and there had been some truly dreadful investments, all of which I had then to deal with."

Lady Henrietta barely glanced at him, her head lowering just a little as her eyes darted to his for a moment.

"I see. That must have been a very difficult time for you."

Touched by her sympathy, Oliver nodded.

"It was. Very difficult indeed, I would say. That being said, it also gave me the determination to do all that I could to make certain that my fortune was soon restored to me."

"That is good."

Lady Henrietta threw him another look, but then turned her gaze away again. Was she embarrassed by what he was saying? For a moment, Oliver thought to stop, to change the subject entirely, but after a moment, he chose to continue.

"My father was not the very best of gentlemen when it came to his coin," he said, taking a deep breath as a flash of pain struck him as he remembered his shock at seeing the state of the estate finances, as well as trying to cope with the grief which had almost entirely overwhelmed him. "Therefore, what the *ton* said of me was, for some time, quite true. I *was* without a good deal of coin, I *was* impoverished." He threw out his chest, a sense of happiness filling him as he smiled at her. "Though that is no longer true." Lady Henrietta sniffed. Oliver blinked, his smile cracking. "That is to say, I have no longer any concern as regards my fortune nor my estates," he said, a little confused by her reaction, wondering why she appeared to be so disinclined to what he was trying to explain. "There is no concern any longer. My investments have done well, the estate will soon have all of the repairs that it required completed, and all shall be well."

"I am glad to hear it."

To Oliver's mind, Lady Henrietta could not have sounded more disinterested if she had tried. His words dried up, his tongue felt a little too big for his mouth and he swallowed thickly, looking away from her. What else was he to say? He had thought that this conversation would be a little more difficult than it had been, though now he was left wondering why she did not seem to have anything to say on all that he had revealed. He had been open with her, vulnerable in speaking as he had done, and yet, Lady Henrietta had only sniffed and murmured a few words. There were no questions, no real relief that things were now as he had said, and that confused him utterly.

"Lady Henrietta?"

She looked up at him again, a vague smile on her face.

"Yes?"

"You seem... distracted." Choosing again to be honest with her, Oliver watched her face, seeing the way that her eyes rounded and her mouth opened just a fraction. "I have spoken to you of a serious matter and yet, you do not appear to have the least bit of interest in it. Surely you must know that I have particular intentions, should all go well between us! I must wonder at your lack of remark over what I have shared."

Lady Henrietta opened and then closed her mouth again, swallowing hard as she gazed up at him.

And then, she closed her eyes.

"Forgive me, Lord Edenbridge," she whispered, hoarsely. "I am not meant to speak of this, but it is my father."

"Your father?"

She nodded and when her eyes opened, there were tears there.

"I have heard that he has gambled a great deal of our fortune away," she whispered, leaning closer to him as sympathy poured into Oliver's heart, leaving him a little embarrassed that he had spoken so bluntly when it was now clear that she was in some sort of distress. "I am sure that it will push a good many gentlemen away from me and, truth be told, Lord Edenbridge, I can understand if you do not wish to even be *connected* with me in any way, any longer."

Oliver shook his head.

"I shall not step away from you, Lady Henrietta, simply because of your father's gambling. I would not do such a thing!"

"But my family might well be just as impoverished as

you once were!" she answered, blinking quickly to push the tears away. "I will bring no income in with me, I will barely have a dowry, if what has been said of my father proves to be true. What then?"

Pausing for a moment as he thought, Oliver then smiled briefly.

"Lady Henrietta, given all that I have endured myself, all that I have had to suffer as a result of my own father's foolishness, I can well understand what you have said, and the pain that you must be enduring. Rest assured, I will not end our acquaintance because of this. And it may prove not to be as bad as you have heard! It may prove to be quite the opposite."

Lady Henrietta closed her eyes and let out a shuddering breath, just as a tear dropped to her cheek.

"I do not think that it will be," she answered, tremulously. "I fear that it will be worse than what we have been told!"

"Even if it is, then you are not without hope," Oliver told her, firmly. "I am sure—"

"How can you say such a thing?" Lady Henrietta interrupted him, her voice loud now, loud with fear and upset. "You have seen how the *ton* turned from you because of your lack of fortune, have you not? I am sure that it will be the same for me! You cannot reassure me, Lord Edenbridge, for I am all too aware of what will happen."

Trying to find something to say, Oliver let out a slow breath, recognizing that what she said was quite true. The *ton* would turn their back on the family, even on those who had done nothing to deserve their censure. Lady Henrietta would find herself without a future, without hope.

He hesitated. *I could court her. I do not care about what her father has done, nor do I care about the size of her dowry.*

Opening his mouth to say that very thing, Oliver's heart squeezed tight, refusing to let those words fall. Frowning, he cleared his throat, seeing Lady Henrietta searching his face, perhaps hoping for some wonderful promise that would solve all of her difficulties.

"Lady Henrietta," he began, still uncertain about what he ought to say now, and wondering why the thought of courting her sent his heart tumbling low. "I am sure – ah! Lord Dunstable, good afternoon! How pleasant to see you."

His friend bowed towards Lady Henrietta though, as he lifted his head, a somewhat quizzical look was sent in Oliver's direction, indicating that perhaps he was a little surprised at how glad Oliver seemed to be to be welcoming him into their company. Perhaps he thought that Oliver wanted nothing more than to be alone with Lady Henrietta when, much to Oliver's surprise, it was a welcome relief to have his friend present.

"Good afternoon," Lord Dunstable said, directing the words towards Lady Henrietta. "I do hope that I have not interrupted you?"

Lady Henrietta blinked, closed her eyes, and then broke into sobs, her gloved hands covering her face and Lord Dunstable immediately took a step back, a panicked look coming into his eyes.

"Lady Henrietta has been telling me about some difficult news regarding her father," Oliver explained, feeling a little helpless and wondering if he ought to put his arm around the young lady's shoulders. He glanced behind him, wondering if her mother was present and willing to come to her daughter's aid, but the lady was herself engrossed in conversation with another lady near them. "Lord Dunstable has long been acquainted with your family, has he not?" When the lady nodded, Oliver gestured to his friend, hoping that Lord Dunstable might find the words to reassure her. "Then you know that he is an excellent fellow and will not share a word of your present difficulty to the *ton*, I can assure you."

"Certainly, I will not!"

Lord Dunstable pulled out a handkerchief from his pocket and handed it to Lady Henrietta, making Oliver realize that he ought to have done such a thing himself. He glanced at Oliver who shrugged lightly, and spread out his hands, silently asking his friend to help him calm the lady. Lord Dunstable gave a small nod and then looked again at the lady, who was now dabbing at her eyes.

"If you wish, you may tell me all of it, Lady Henrietta."

Lord Dunstable glanced again at Oliver, who spoke quickly.

"I have no doubt that Lord Dunstable will be just as reassuring as I have been. Mayhap that might encourage you?"

Lady Henrietta sniffed, keeping the handkerchief clasped tightly in her hand, her eyes, damp with tears, looking up towards Lord Dunstable.

"All I want to know is whether or not you would step away from me also, Lord Dunstable," she said, her voice a mournful whisper. "Lord Edenbridge says that he will not, but I am fearful that so many others will."

Lord Dunstable frowned and then leaned closer to her.

"Whatever has happened, Lady Henrietta?"

"Lord Edenbridge?"

Oliver turned his head, just to see Lady Harsham and Lady Guilford coming towards him, a warm smile spreading across both their faces.

"We thought to come and speak to you but alas, I fear that we have broken you apart!" Lady Guilford exclaimed, making Oliver turn his head to see Lord Dunstable and Lady Henrietta walking away from them, with Lord Dunstable's head close to Lady Henrietta's.

"I am glad that you thought to be so kind," he answered with a smile. "Lord Dunstable is a friend of Lady Henrietta's family, I believe, for they have all been acquainted with each other for many a year." His smile slipped. "Alas, Lady Henrietta has had some difficult news thrust upon her, and our pleasant walk turned into something quite sorrowful indeed." He looked again to where his friend was walking with the lady, a sense of relief in his chest. "Lord Dunstable will know what to say. I was not able to offer anything to her, I am afraid."

A frown began to pull at his forehead as he remembered how close he had come to asking to court her, only for his heart to pull him back. Why had it been so fierce in its determination to drag him away from her? She was someone that he was considering, was she not? She was lovely, kind, and excellent in her conversation and manner, and he was certainly fond of her, at the very least. So why, when it came to it, had he been so unwilling to offer her courtship?

"Lord Edenbridge? Are you quite all right?" Lady Harsham touched his arm. "You have gone very quiet and are scowling as though you have thought of something displeasing!"

Oliver blinked rapidly and then shook his head as though to cast the expression from his face.

"I am quite well, forgive me. It is concern only. Given what Lady Henrietta has told me, I am now very well aware of what she will face and that it is going to be a very difficult situation indeed." Sighing, he rubbed one hand over his chin. "I only hope that she will find the strength to overcome it all."

"With good friends such as Lord Dunstable beside her, as well as your support – and the support from others, such as myself and Lady Guilford – I am sure that, whatever has happened, she will be encouraged."

Lady Harsham smiled, and Oliver nodded, her words of comfort touching his heart.

"I think that you are quite correct." With a deep breath, he gestured towards Lady Henrietta and Lord Dunstable. "I had thought to offer to court her the very moment that she told me of her troubles, but Lord Dunstable interrupted me before I could do so." Wincing, he saw Lady Guilford and Lady Harsham exchange a look. "It came from a desire to aid her, I suppose, though I am glad that I did not say anything. I have still Miss Leverton to consider, and I have not yet spoken with her about my fortune, as I have been advised to do. I can see now that it would have been an impulsive decision, had I offered courtship to Lady Henrietta." With a quiet laugh, he ran one hand over his eyes. "I ought not to have said anything to you either, I am sure, for now I have only brought shame to myself!"

Lady Harsham smiled, but dropped her gaze and, instead, took his arm.

"There is no shame in wishing to save someone from whatever difficulty they find themselves in."

"I quite agree," Lady Guilford agreed, as they all fell into step together. "Though I think we should hurry to catch Lady Henrietta and Lord Dunstable before her mother notices that she is walking with another!"

Laughing, Oliver pushed aside his embarrassment and began to walk, noticing that there was no concern in his heart over the fact that Lord Dunstable was now arm in arm with Lady Henrietta.

Looking to his right and seeing Lady Harsham there made him quite contented and, with a soft smile on his face, he hurried after the others.

CHAPTER SIXTEEN

*J*ane tried not to look at Lady Guilford as they meandered back to their carriage. All the same, she could feel the intensity of her friend's gaze, knowing exactly what was on the lady's mind, but having no real desire to speak of it, not when her thoughts were already as tormented as they were.

"Jane. Please."

With a sigh, Jane finally turned her gaze to Lady Guilford.

"I know what you want to ask me."

"You do?"

"Of course I do."

Lady Guilford frowned.

"But you will not speak of it, then? Is it because you have no wish to?"

"It is because I do not know what I feel!" Jane threw up her hands, letting out an exasperated breath which, in turn, brought Lady Guilford to a complete stop, her eyes a little wider now. "The feelings which swept through me when I heard that he had been about to ask to court Lady Henrietta were so strong, I have still not quite settled even now! An hour after hearing those words on his lips, I cannot find a single moment of calmness."

Lady Guilford smiled gently, her eyes holding fast to Jane's.

"But do you not feel glad, at least, that he did *not* do such a thing? That he did *not* suggest courtship?"

Jane nodded but closed her eyes, aware of the heat there.

"It is foolishness, Louisa. I have already determined that I will not seek out another husband, I have already told myself that I am quite contented just as I am." Her eyes opened but a single tear fell to her cheek, though Jane quickly dashed it away. "You have told me that Lord Edenbridge is the exact opposite of my late husband in terms of his character, and I believe you, I do, but there is a part of me that is still very afraid."

"And so, you think it best to set aside your feelings and encourage Lord Edenbridge in the direction of another?" It was a question that Jane could not answer. Part of her wanted to say yes, to agree that it would be better for him to marry someone else, while the other part of her heart cried out in dismay, begging her to tell him all in the hope that she might find a new happiness with him. "Jane." Lady Guilford put a hand to Jane's arm as fresh tears began to push themselves forward. "You must be honest with him, as I have told you already. Tell him everything."

"I have." Jane squeezed her eyes closed, then shook her head. "I do not mean that. That is to say, I have said a little about Lord Harsham to him."

"And was he understanding?"

Nodding, Jane's heart squeezed all over again.

"Yes, he was. *More* than understanding, if I am to be

honest. He told me that he felt honored by my willingness to be so honest with him about something so personal and, in that regard, I felt my heart fill all the more with joy and happiness about his friendship."

"Tell him everything," Lady Guilford said, with a firm yet gentle tone. "You know that I care about you, my dear friend, and I can see that this chance for happiness is one that you will forever regret the loss of, if you do not pursue it. Trust your heart, in a way that you have not done before."

Jane sniffed.

"I have never had a chance to trust my heart before, I suppose," she said quietly, the idea beginning to soften in her mind, no longer as brash a thought as before. "But then, if I do so, I will have to tell him about The London Chronicle also."

"And that will make him think all the more highly of you!" Lady Guilford beamed at Jane, though doubt still swarmed in her mind. "He will not turn from you because of that!"

"There is a chance that he might."

Lady Guilford shook her head.

"No. He has spoken of just how much he values the advice he has been given, has he not? I cannot imagine that he would think ill of you for keeping that from him. Rather, he will be all the more grateful for your willingness to assist him, both anonymously and also as a friend."

Another clutch of fear tugged at Jane's heart, rather than bringing her any sort of comfort.

"He might think that I have deceived him!"

Lady Guilford grasped Jane's hand, hard, startling her out of the fear which threatened to overwhelm her.

"Do not let the whispers of dread and doubt succeed in their attempts to steal this potential happiness from you."

Jane blinked rapidly, her tears still very present. "I know Lord Edenbridge a little, but I have seen how close you have become to him and how much he admires you!" her friend continued, no sense of irritation present but a steadiness all the same; a steadiness which demanded Jane's full attention. "I can see how he smiles when you come to join him, how light leaps into his eyes at the sight of you. Did you not see how he spoke of Lady Henrietta?"

A little confused, Jane frowned.

"I heard his explanation of why he had not done what he had first thought to do, that is all."

"But he did not seem upset by it, did he?" Lady Guilford's eyes searched Jane's face, as though she was silently praying that she would understand. "Lord Edenbridge was relieved that he had said nothing! He did not seem upset that he had missed his opportunity, nor sorrowful that he had decided against it. There was no sense of frustration or the like, and nor did he seem in the least bit concerned about Lord Dunstable and Lady Henrietta walking together."

"Lord Dunstable?"

"Yes, Lord Dunstable!" A glint came into Lady Guilford's eyes. "If that gentleman truly cared for Lady Henrietta, even a little, then I know for certain that he would not have been standing conversing with us while the lady he was courting then was on the arm of another! If he had any genuine interest in her, he would have hurried to join them, to stop the intimate conversation as quickly as he could." It was not something that Jane had considered before. She frowned, then looked away, a flare of hope striking her square in the chest. "You will only be able to understand all that you feel if you accept that there is a possibility of happiness with Lord Edenbridge," Lady Guilford said, a good deal more gently now. "And thereafter, you must tell him of it all – of your hesitation, your fears, your doubts, and your desires. Then you will be able not only to ascertain his reaction and response to what you say, but also what his own heart feels. You can trust him with this, Jane. I am sure of it."

Jane closed her eyes, swaying just a little as she took a long breath, attempting to steady herself.

"I – I will think about it, Louisa."

"That is good. I will not press you any more than I have already done... only to say that you might wish to tell him at the masquerade ball, for there is something a good deal easier about speaking of such things when one is wearing a mask!"

This made Jane laugh, albeit rather ruefully as she understood exactly what her friend meant.

"Mayhap," was all she would say though, as she made her way home, she could think of nothing else but Lord Edenbridge and the chance she might dare take... were she bold enough.

~

"GOOD EVENING!"

Jane swept into a curtsey, her heart hammering furiously as she looked up at Lord Edenbridge, his eyes hidden behind a small mask – though it was nowhere near large enough to hide his true identity.

"Good evening, Lord Edenbridge. Thank you for your invitation."

She kept her voice a little higher pitched than usual, an idea having come to her that she might soon follow through with, should she have the strength of mind and heart to do so.

Lord Edenbridge frowned, though his lips still curved.

"A lady I do not recognize," he said, with a sudden chuckle. "But you must be one of my acquaintances, I am sure!"

"I am indeed." Jane swallowed tightly, leaning a little closer. "We are acquainted enough to send letters upon occasion, Lord Edenbridge."

This made his frown deepen, only for his eyebrows to lift high, an expression of understanding suddenly overtaking his face.

"Wait," he breathed, his hand reaching out to catch hers, "do you mean to say—"

"Good *evening*, Lord Edenbridge!"

The lady behind Jane, one who was clearly eager to have her presence made known, stepped closer to him, and quickly, the conversation was brought to an end. Lord Edenbridge dropped Jane's hand and, as propriety demanded of him, bowed low and smiled at his next guest. Jane made her way to the door of the ballroom, glancing behind her only to see Lord Edenbridge looking towards her at the same time – and a flush of heat began to rise up from the tips of her toes. With what she hoped was a smile – though it could have been her nervousness twisting her lips – Jane made her way into the ballroom, hopeful now that Lord Edenbridge would come in search of her soon. She had made sure that the mask she wore was obvious enough, with some small peacock feathers pressing outwards from either side. She had asked her maid to thread pearls through her hair and then to add two larger peacock feathers to the back of her hair, again hoping to make herself memorable to Lord Edenbridge.

I must only hope that, when the time comes, I have the strength to speak.

"Jane! There you are."

Jane turned her head and then practically fell on the arm of Lady Guilford.

"I have done it."

"You... you have?" Lady Guilford frowned. "What have you done?"

"I have told him that I write for The London Chronicle," Jane breathed, pressing one hand hard against her stomach, hoping to calm the nerves that swirled through her. "He does not know that it is me, under this mask, of course, but all the same, I have told him in the hope that he will come and find me. Then, I will be able to tell him."

Lady Guilford frowned, turned to face Jane, and then spread out her hands.

"I do not understand."

Jane swallowed tightly.

"I came with my true appearance hidden, as you can see." She gestured to herself. "You knew the mask I was to wear and the gown and the hairpiece and thus, you recognized me, but Lord Edenbridge did not. I did not tell him who I was, I lifted my voice a little, and I whispered to him that we knew one another through letters."

"Ah." Understanding made Lady Guilford's whole expression lift. "And now you intend to tell him the truth?" When Jane nodded, Lady Guilford leaned forward, one eyebrow lifting. "*All* of it?"

"I – I do not know," Jane stammered, still a little confused. "I confess to you that I have had some time to think but, no matter how much I tell myself that all will be well and that he can be trusted, there is still a vast part of me that is uncertain and afraid." She swallowed tightly, spreading out her hands. "It may be that when the time comes, I will feel able to say it all but, until that moment, I remain unsure."

Lady Guilford nodded.

"I understand. Though I am glad to see that you are being bold, my dear friend. I think it will do you very well."

"Ladies, have you heard the news?"

"News?" Lady Guilford frowned as a lady that Jane did not recognize hurried close, her eyes bright in a way that Jane did not much like. "If this is to be gossip, Lady Smithing, then I am not sure that—"

"Miss Leverton has eloped!"

Jane's mouth fell open in utter astonishment, though she quickly tried to rearrange her expression of surprise into something more akin to displeasure at being told such a thing. She did not want to hear gossip, but at the same time, there was a desire within her to know more about what had happened to Miss Leverton. The last time she had spoken to Lord Edenbridge about the lady, there had been no hint of any other gentleman even showing an interest in her, so to hear now that she had eloped was nothing short of astonishing.

"Eloped?" Lady Guilford, despite her clear dislike of gossip, showed the same amount of surprise in her expression as Jane felt. "When did this happen?"

"Only yesterday! Though we have only just heard of it now. I did not think that Miss Leverton was the sort of young lady to ever be snatched away by such a fellow, but it seems as though she is!"

"And who is the gentleman?" Jane could not help but ask, seeing Lady Smithing's smile grow just a little. "I do hope that he is worthy of her and not some rogue."

"He is no rogue!" Lady Smithing answered, laughing,

though Jane did not know why. "He is the dullest, most severe gentleman in all of London, I think! A gentleman by the name of Lord Whittington."

This meant nothing to Jane, though from Lady Guilford, the name brought a gasp of surprise.

"Indeed!" Lady Smithing chuckled, shaking her head. "But despite his disinclination to balls, soirées, and the like, despite his seemingly hard demeanor, he has swept her off to be married in Scotland!"

Jane exchanged a look with Lady Guilford, wondering silently now if Miss Leverton's quiet manner and continual glances toward her mother had all been a pretense. Had she been pretending to be demure, quiet, and severely under her mother's rule, so that no one would suspect her interest in this Lord Whittington? Or had it been a single look, a single meeting which had changed her entirely, and practically forced her steps in a direction she would not otherwise have taken?

"I am sure that her mother will be quite upset," Lady Guilford murmured, as Lady Smithing's eyes began to search all around the room, perhaps looking for the next group of people she might share this with. "I am sure that—"

"Yes, yes, quite." With a vague smile, Lady Smithing waved one hand in Lady Guilford's direction and then took her leave. "Do excuse me now, will you?"

It was not as though Jane had any opportunity to ask her to linger, given just how quickly she took her leave. Certain that there was still a look of surprise etched on her face, she spread out her hands as Lady Guilford shook her head.

"Goodness," Lady Guilford breathed, as Jane's hands dropped back to her sides. "What an extraordinary thing to hear!"

"I quite agree. I would never have imagined that Miss Leverton was the type of young lady to do such a thing!"

Lady Guilford looked at her, a slight frown on her forehead.

"Are you going to speak with him?"

Confused, Jane blinked.

"Speak with whom?"

"With Lord Edenbridge," Lady Guilford said, quickly. "He must be told! You do not want him to hear it from someone else, do you? That would be a little embarrassing for him, I am sure, for whoever tells him might well be seeking his reaction in the hope of spreading that as yet more gossip."

"I had not thought of that."

"But you must tell him as yourself, must you not?"

Frowning, Jane tried to understand.

"What do you mean?"

"Well, the lady who writes for The London Chronicle does not know the specific ladies that he was pursuing, does she?"

Understanding what her friend meant, a shuddering breath ran through Jane's frame as she looked down at her gown, recalling the peacock feathers in her hair and the mask that she had been so sure he would notice and remember.

"And if I go to speak with him about Miss Leverton specifically, he will wonder how I know of it all."

"It could be that he would simply accept that you know of it because you are a part of the *ton* and have observed him," Lady Guilford said, though Jane shook her head at this, quite certain that it would not satisfy him.

"I am going to have to tell him." Her eyes squeezed closed, a tight fear beginning to crawl over her skin, delving down deep into her soul. "I am going to have to tell him everything."

"Just as you had planned."

"But not like this," Jane answered, a little hoarsely. "I thought I would have time to consider what I was going to say, and would be given the opportunity to build up my courage! Now I am going to have to go to him directly and speak all of my truth all at once!"

Lady Guilford took Jane's hand and pressed it, leaning a little closer to her.

"You might find that it will be better this way," she said, encouraging Jane just a little, though her fear still remained strong. "It is clear even in this just how much you have come to care for him, my friend. Let *that* – your affection – be your guide. The rest will come."

Jane could only nod and then, before her courage failed her entirely, turned on her heel and went in search of Lord Edenbridge.

CHAPTER SEVENTEEN

*W*here is she?

The lady with the peacock feathers adorning both her hair and her mask had caught Oliver's attention from the very moment that she had smiled at him. There had been something very familiar about her, though he had not recognized her voice. It was when she had spoken to him, however, when she had whispered those words about sharing letters that he had finally realized who she was – the writer for The London Chronicle! He had wanted to capture her hand and her attention, to tell her of his gratitude, of his overwhelming appreciation for all that she had done to help guide him but, yet, due to his responsibilities as host, he had been forced to let her go. Now, however, he was determined to find her.

"Edenbridge."

Oliver glanced to his left, just as a hand caught his elbow.

"Yes?"

"It is I." The gentleman spread out his hands, sounding

a little exasperated when Oliver did not immediately recognize him. "Dunstable."

"Good evening, Dunstable." Oliver chuckled, though his eyes continued to rove around the room. "I did not recognize you with such an... ornate mask on." He glanced at his friend again, taking in the silver mask which covered half of one side of his face as well as both eyes. "It is as though you do not wish to be seen!"

Lord Dunstable did not smile.

"I must speak with you."

The smile fixed itself to Oliver's face as he heard the seriousness in his friend's voice.

"We *are* speaking, are we not?"

"In private." Oliver blinked. "Now, if you please."

"Now?" Oliver gestured to the room. "My friend, I am hosting this evening! I have many people present and all of them—"

Lord Dunstable grasped Oliver's arm, hard.

"*Please.* I would not ask if it was not of the greatest importance."

Considering this, Oliver set aside his desire to find the lady with the peacock feathers in her hair and instead, relented so that he might go to speak with his friend.

"Very well."

Lord Dunstable relaxed outwardly, his hand no longer gripping so hard, his shoulders dropping and a long breath escaping him.

"I thank you. This way, if you please."

Oliver followed after his friend as Lord Dunstable made his way through the crowd and then, much to Oliver's surprise, out into the hallway. Thereafter, he stepped into Oliver's parlor with a familiarity that came with them having been such good friends for so many years.

The moment that Oliver stepped into the room, however, shock hit him with such force that he stumbled back. There, waiting for them with her hands clasped directly in front of her, was none other than Lady Henrietta. She did not wear a mask, holding it instead by its ribbons, and her eyes were already sparkling with tears – though what had caused them, Oliver did not know.

His shock quickly turned to anger.

"Whatever are you doing?" he hissed, coming close to Lord Dunstable, his hand grasping his arm, tightly. "You cannot have Lady Henrietta waiting here alone! Where is her mother? Or any sort of chaperone? I know that her family is in some sort of difficulty but that does not mean that you can force my arm!"

"Force your arm?" Lord Dunstable repeated, puzzlement on his face, only for it to clear in an instant as he shook off Oliver's hand. "That is *not* what I brought you here for, my friend! Surely you know me better than that?"

Oliver's confusion and anger began to fade as he searched his friend's face. After a moment, he released Lord Dunstable's arm and then closed his eyes as he let out a small sigh.

"You are a worthy gentleman," he muttered, reaching around to take off his mask. "You would never force my hand, I know. I should not have suggested that." He opened his eyes. "My sincere apologies."

"I thank you." Lord Dunstable let out a slow breath. "My friend, I asked you here so that we might speak together – all of us."

Looking at Lady Henrietta and seeing how she pulled her handkerchief from her sleeve to dab at her eyes, Oliver frowned.

"What is this about?"

"It is to do with Lady Henrietta and her family," Lord Dunstable answered. "You know that I have long been acquainted with them all and I must say, to hear what her father has done makes me greatly concerned for Lady Henrietta's future."

"I am sorry to hear that." Keeping his voice quiet, Oliver looked back at Lady Henrietta, just as she brought her gaze to his. "It is as you feared, then."

Lady Henrietta's voice wobbled.

"It is. Though it is even worse than I was first told."

Oliver waited to see if the urge to offer to court the lady rose up within him but instead, what came to him was a vision of Lady Harsham. It was most unexpected and took Oliver quite by surprise, making him shake his head to himself – though Lady Henrietta clearly took it to be his reaction to what *she* had said to him.

"It is quite dreadful," she said, her voice breaking now. "I did not know what I was to do, quite certain that my future was bleak." Her gaze drifted towards Lord Dunstable. "But then Lord Dunstable and I spoke and... well..."

"That is when I determined that we had to speak with you." Lord Dunstable cleared his throat, his gaze dropping, a sudden tension seeming to flood through his frame. "I hope that you will understand. I do not want to make you angry or upset you in any way."

Thoroughly confused, Oliver looked from one to the other.

"Why should I be angry?"

"Because I know that you were thinking of courting me," Lady Henrietta answered, still looking to Lord Dunstable. "I was sure that you would turn from me once you had heard about my father, but Lord Dunstable reassured me."

A small, wry smile touched Lord Dunstable's lips.

"I reassured her, to the point that I realized that I would not be very pleased if you were to court her, Edenbridge."

A knot forming at his brows, Oliver's jaw set tight.

"Why ever not?"

"Because," Lord Dunstable answered, reaching out one hand to the lady, "because I have realized that *I* wish to do so."

"You... you wish to court Lady Henrietta?" Oliver blinked furiously as Lord Dunstable nodded, glancing at the lady in question and then looking back to Oliver. "*You*, who have known her for such a long time but never once thought to do so before?"

Lord Dunstable nodded, closing his eyes.

"Perhaps it is because I have known her for so long that I did not realize what was truly within my heart."

"I... we do not want you to be angry with us," Lady Henrietta whispered, though she drew closer to Lord Dunstable. "We wanted you to know of our hopes before we made any approach to my father or mother."

"I intend to obtain a Special License," Lord Dunstable added, quickly. "It is not just courtship that I am considering, my friend. It is much, much more than that."

"I can see that." Oliver considered this for a few moments, a little surprised that he felt nothing but delight at this news. "My dear friend, though I am astonished, I confess that I am quite delighted to know that you want to court the lady... forgive me, to *marry* the lady."

Lord Dunstable blinked rapidly, clearly surprised at the easy way in which Oliver had taken this news.

"You – you are?"

"I am." Oliver moved closer and then took Lady Henrietta's hand. "I am delighted to know that you have found a gentleman who will do nothing other than care for you just as you deserve. I know that you have been acquainted with Lord Dunstable for a long while and if it is that you have both truly found a new sense of happiness in your connection, then I certainly will not stand in the way of that. Instead, I will encourage it!"

Lady Henrietta's eyes filled with tears all over again, though she smiled more brightly than Oliver had ever seen before.

"Thank you, Lord Edenbridge. You are truly a considerate, kind, and caring gentleman and I have been grateful for your company."

"You are most welcome." Oliver looked to Lord Dunstable and then shook his hand, firmly. "And to you, my friend, might I offer my most sincere congratulations?"

Lord Dunstable smiled, though he appeared a little dazed, almost as though he could not quite take in all that Oliver had said.

"I – I thank you, my friend."

"If there is to be opportunity to join you on your wedding day, I hope you know that I would find it a privilege to be present."

"I thank you." Lord Dunstable glanced at his bride. "It will depend on just how quickly we need to marry. I do not want Lady Henrietta to suffer any more than she has already done, and news of her father's foolishness has not yet spread through the *ton*... though it will not be long."

"I quite understand." Putting one hand to his heart, Oliver bowed to them both. "And thank you for your consideration in speaking to me so openly about these things. I am truly grateful."

"I am only glad that your heart was not injured," Lord Dunstable answered, sounding more relieved now. "Your understanding has made this matter a good deal easier."

"But of course." Gesturing to the door, Oliver smiled as Lady Henrietta quickly put her mask back on again, only to then take the arm of Lord Dunstable. "I am truly delighted for you both."

Watching them walk from the room, Oliver closed the door but then leaned back against it, choosing not to go into the ballroom immediately thereafter. Though he was not upset by the news, it had been something of a shock to hear that Lord Dunstable now considered himself practically in love with Lady Henrietta and intended to marry her! Trying to let the news sink in a little more, Oliver closed his eyes and let out a long, slow breath.

I do not feel any sorrow nor sadness about this, he reminded himself, astonished as a slight relief began to flood his chest. *I did not even think of Lady Henrietta in all of this. The only person I thought of was Lady Harsham.*

Oliver closed his eyes and rested his head back against the door, breathing deeply. There was something strong in his connection with Lady Harsham, he had to admit it. But was there something more there than just mere friendship?

His eyes popped open as a sudden thought struck him.

Have I been so caught up in my pursuit of two other young ladies that I missed what was directly in front of my eyes?

Letting out a slow breath, Oliver pushed himself away from the door, realizing that, as yet, he had not greeted Lady Harsham – or mayhap he had without realizing it. Had he been so busy thinking about the lady with the peacock feathers that he had not recognized her when she had first arrived? A trifle irritated with himself, Oliver strode back to the ballroom and pulled open the door, determined now to go in search of Lady Harsham – though quite how he was to find her at a masquerade ball, he did not know!

"Lord Edenbridge?"

Turning his head, Oliver's heart clattered in his chest.

"My Lady." He went to hurry forward, only for the lady, her peacock feathers bobbing in her hair as she moved, to reach for his arm to hold him in place.

"Might we speak?" she asked, catching his hand very briefly, but in a way that spoke of familiarity. "It is important, Lord Edenbridge."

Oliver frowned, struggling to hear her over the sound of the ballroom which was growing loud and raucous.

"You wish to speak with me?"

"Now."

It was said with the same urgency as Lord Dunstable had spoken and, all the more confused, Oliver permitted the lady to lead him out into the hallway, aware of the knot which tied itself in his stomach.

"Lord Edenbridge." The lady released his arm, then spread out her hands. "I have come to tell you of some rumors which I have heard. I believe that they are true rather than rumor, however, though I am sorry to have to tell you of it."

"Rumors?" The word sent a buzzing into Oliver's ears, memories of all he had already endured throwing themselves at him. "What have you heard?"

The lady hesitated for a moment, then took a breath.

"I have been told that Miss Leverton has eloped with a gentleman by the name of Lord Whittington." Oliver gaped at her, shock ricocheting through him. "I know that it must be a great shock to you, but I did not want you to hear of it from another, who might then look to spread news of your reaction to others. It is known to some in the *ton*, at least, that you have been showing an interest in the lady."

For some minutes, Oliver could say nothing. It was not

that he had become overly interested in Miss Leverton and was eager to have more of her company, nor that he found himself upset that she had turned away from him so quickly. It was simply the astonishment of hearing that she had done such a thing, for the lady he had come to know was quiet, reserved, and under the severe gaze of her mother at all times. Never would he have imagined that she had such boldness!

"I am sorry."

It was the softness of her hand on his that made Oliver start in surprise, tugging him out of his thoughts. He looked down into the lady's eyes, trying to sort out his many, complicated thoughts.

"You are very considerate, my Lady." A broken, jerking laugh issued from his lips. "It seems that I have lost two young ladies on the same evening! No doubt you have also heard that I was considering Lady Henrietta, yes?" He looked away from her as the lady nodded, feeling a sense of foolishness wash over him. "My closest friend is now to marry her, though I cannot say that I am in any way upset or angry about that. To see them together, to see the hope that they now had, did make my heart glad." He closed his eyes briefly. "For myself, however, it now seems that I shall, yet again, garner the attention of the *ton*, though they will most likely do nothing but laugh at me this time."

"I am sure it is not so."

"Oh, but it shall be," Oliver replied, a little more gruffly than he had intended, heat beginning to build in his chest. "I can already hear their sharp tongues speaking of me, telling all of their friends and acquaintances that I am a gentleman who can never garner the attention of a young lady for long." Letting out a long sigh, he closed his eyes. "I suppose it does not matter. Mayhap I ought not to have come to London this Season."

"Do not say that." The tenderness in her voice made Oliver's eyes open, a slight frown flicking across his forehead as he looked back at the lady, still trying to ascertain who she was. "There is still hope."

"Hope?" Oliver shook his head. "No, my Lady. Despite your best attempts to help me – help which I have highly valued and wanted to thank you for – it seems as though I have lost the interest of both ladies that I have been considering. There can be no hope with either of them although, I should say, I do not find myself greatly sorrowful over it." Quite why he was telling her such things, Oliver did not know, but there was something about their connection – albeit through letter writing only – that made him feel as though he could be quite open with her. "But I do thank you for your desire to come and tell me about Miss Leverton before someone in the *ton* thought to do so."

"I am relieved that I caught you before it was spoken of to you by another," came the answer, a softness in her tone that made Oliver's breath catch, a little unsure as to why he felt such a strength in his connection to the lady when he had never met her in person before. "Lord Edenbridge, I must ask you... that is, I must tell you–"

"Ah, Lord Edenbridge! There you are."

The door swung open, and Oliver turned quickly, seeing a gentleman by the name of Lord Tertford hurry towards him. Inwardly, he groaned, seeing the broad grin on the gentleman's face, quite sure he knew why the man was smiling.

"Lord Tertford," he began, turning back so that he might introduce the lady with the peacock feathers in her hair – even though he did not know her name – only to see an empty space where she had been standing. "I – yes, well." Clearing his throat, he forced a smile. "You have come, no doubt, to inform me that Miss Leverton has eloped, yes?"

The smile on Lord Tertford's face immediately began to fade.

"Well, yes, that was what I had come to speak to you about. But you are already aware of it, it seems."

Oliver kept his smile pinned in place.

"Yes, I am. Though it is no great sorrow to me."

"No?" Lord Tertford's expression grew into one of astonishment. "I am surprised. I would have thought that you might be brokenhearted! After all, it was clear to some of us that you were interested in pursuing the lady, but now, it seems, she is gone from you and that can no longer be!"

"I am well used to being rejected," Oliver answered, in what he hoped was a somewhat careless tone. "This is simply another who does not think well of me, I suppose."

"And is there any other that you might turn to?"

Oliver frowned, seeing the glint which came into the gentleman's eye. He certainly was not about to admit anything to him!

"I have been giving a good deal of my time to Miss Leverton, as you are aware," he said, omitting any mention of Lady Henrietta for fear that the gentleman had not heard about his interest in that lady also. "I have not had time nor desire to pursue any other and therefore, I can tell you quite truthfully that I have no one else in mind." He let out what he hoped sounded like a small, melancholy sigh. "Indeed, I think that I shall now enjoy the rest of the Season without pursuing any young lady and, thereafter, make my way back to my estate. Mayhap next Season, I shall find myself a little more fortunate!"

"Indeed." Lord Tertford offered a small, wry smile, but to Oliver's eyes, clearly looked a little disappointed which, in turn, brought him a good deal of relief. With any luck, this would turn the gentleman from him entirely and there would be no more gossip spread about him. "There is always hope, Lord Edenbridge."

With an insincere smile, Lord Tertford bowed and then stepped back towards the ballroom door, leaving Oliver to follow. He did glance over his shoulder, wondering where the lady with the peacock feathers had gone, but he could see not even the smallest glimpse of her. A little frustrated that their conversation had come to an end so quickly before it had even begun, Oliver made his way back into the ballroom, no longer as happy nor as contented as he had been at the start.

CHAPTER EIGHTEEN

"You must tell me why you are so melancholy." Jane could only smile briefly as she walked, arm in arm, with Lady Guilford. She could not give her any answer, for her heart was too pained and sore for her to speak freely. "You did not tell Lord Edenbridge the truth, then?" her friend pressed, albeit in a gentle manner. "You did not have the opportunity, or you did not have the courage?"

The words smarted a little, but Jane merely accepted the feeling.

"I did not have the opportunity, though I am not certain that I would have had the courage, should it have come to it."

"Then you must simply tell him now!"

The idea seemed so simple, Jane considered, but it held so much depth, so much *pain,* that she could not even contemplate it.

"No, Louisa. I cannot."

"Why?"

The view of Hyde Park blurred as tears rushed into Jane's vision.

"Please, Louisa." The words were tight and broken, her emotions growing to such a swell that she could not contain them, not even here in public. "I cannot."

"Jane!"

Seemingly astonished by Jane's outward expression of anguish, Lady Guilford stopped walking for a moment, turned to look Jane straight in the eye, and then, after scrutinizing her, led her to a bench nearby. Jane sat obediently, knowing that her friend wanted her to explain, and feeling the desire within her to tell all, in the hope that it might bring her some relief.

"He did not recognize me," she began before Lady Guilford could begin asking questions. "I was going to tell him, truly, I was, but then we were interrupted by another gentleman." She dropped her gaze to her hands resting in her lap, squeezing her eyes closed tightly so that the tears in her eyes would fade just a little. All the same, her breath shuddered out of her, her words shaking as she spoke. "I heard him tell this gentleman that he had no thought of any other, that there was no interest for him in any lady in the *ton*. I hid myself away the moment that this other gentleman arrived, so that he would not see me talking with a gentleman alone, but all the same, I heard everything."

Lady Guilford's expression grew into one of sympathy, and she took Jane's hand, pressing it.

"My dear friend, you cannot be sure that he spoke the truth, can you?"

Jane kept her eyes closed.

"It sounded truthful to me. He said that he would simply enjoy the rest of the Season and then return home to his estate. That does not give me any hope."

Lady Guilford frowned.

"What was the name of this other gentleman?"

"Lord Tertford, I think. I do not know him."

Lady Guilford's expression pulled into a scowl.

"He is not a good fellow, and is known for his inclination to gossip. No doubt he was eager to find Lord Edenbridge and tell him of Miss Leverton, so that he could see his reaction and then gossip about it!" She smiled. "It would be very wise of Lord Edenbridge to remain silent and not to give any truth about himself away to Lord Tertford." Jane opened her eyes, blinking the moisture away from her lashes. "I would not take anything that Lord Edenbridge said to Lord Tertford to be the truth," her friend continued, gently. "He would not be speaking honestly, I am sure of it!"

Considering this, Jane's heart rose just a little, then fell.

"Be that as it may, I am sure that he spoke the truth when it came to his decision just to enjoy the Season and then return home. It seems as though it is not just Miss Leverton who is now unavailable, for Lady Henrietta is now to be wed to Lord Dunstable!" Lady Guilford gasped, her eyes widening. "Lord Dunstable has known the family – and Lady Henrietta – for a long time." Jane offered her friend a small smile. "I am glad for them, and Lord Edenbridge appeared to be quite happy also. Though he did speak of his upset in knowing that the *ton* would soon be laughing at him for losing not one lady from his interest, but two, at almost the same time."

"That is unfortunate, though not for you, I am sure."

Jane threw her friend a look, but then pulled her gaze away, no sense of hope in her heart any longer.

"You think that he may still be harboring an interest in me, Louisa, but I cannot believe you. Not after what he said, not after the heaviness in his voice and his expression. No, I think it might be best to remain silent on my feelings."

"But you had decided to be bold!" her friend exclaimed, releasing Jane's hand. "You had thought to be honest, to see if there might be a chance of happiness for you both!"

Jane's lips curved into a sad smile.

"I think any hope of that has come to an end, Louisa. All that is left for me now is simply to accept it."

'WE ENCLOSE the letters for the upcoming publication'

Jane picked up the three letters which The London Chronicle had sent to her, trying her utmost to keep her thoughts on the letters themselves, rather than on Lord Edenbridge. After her walk with Lady Guilford in the park the previous day, she had returned home with a new sorrow which, since then, she had been unable to shake off. It was as though, in accepting that she would no longer pursue an attempt to tell Lord Edenbridge the truth, she had also accepted the bleak sorrow that would be her future. How strange it was that the future she had always hoped for, one with employment, security, and no need to marry, now seemed so unappealing!

Giving herself a slight shake, Jane opened the first letter and then read it, before setting it aside. It was a simple enough response, one which would instruct the young lady that it *was* wise to continue on with her dancing master, no matter how much she disliked him. Breaking the seal of the second without so much as looking at the front, she unfolded it and then began to read.

For a moment, she did not comprehend the words on the page.

Her heart shuddered with a sudden fright as she continued to read. The words were speaking directly to her, she was sure, but how could he know?

'I write to beg of you to come to speak to me directly. The conversation we began was short and left unfinished, interrupted by a most disagreeable fellow. I said what I had to, to remove him from my company, but then, when I looked for you, you were nowhere to be found. Please, do come to speak with me again. There is much that I want to say, and there is much, I am sure, that you might also wish to share with me. If you do not seek me out, then be assured that I will seek you out instead. I cannot let our connection cease, not when there is so much more to be shared.'

Reading it, Jane trembled violently, then dropped it on the table before she rose to her feet and began to walk back and forth in the room. It *was* Lord Edenbridge, she knew, but he spoke with such fervency that she could not quite understand it! It was as though he was desperate to see her again, desperate to speak with her and desperate to *share* more... though what he meant by that, Jane could not imagine.

"Will I go to him?"

The question hung in the air as she paced back and forth, her heart squeezing, her mind spinning with the questions that poured into it. What would she do? If she went, would he be astonished to see that it was her, then refuse to say what it was he had wanted to share? Or would he be glad to know that it was her?

Closing her eyes, Jane grasped the back of a chair and tipped her head forward, her eyes closing for a moment.

If I do not go to him, he has promised that he will seek me out, she told herself. *One way or the other, he will discover me.*

She swallowed tightly. Might she be bold enough to do as he had asked? Could she find the strength within her to do as he wanted, even though she did not know what might come of it? Closing her eyes, Jane gripped the chair all the harder, lowering her head just a little.

And if I do not, will I regret it, forever?

CHAPTER NINETEEN

"*T*here is something I must tell you."

Oliver blinked as a lady sailed into his study, her eyes bright with passion, her voice seeming to echo around the room. It took him a moment to take her in, such was his surprise.

"Lady... Lady Guilford, good afternoon."

"Yes, yes, yes." She waved a hand, clearly dismissing the formalities. "As I said, there is something that I must tell you. It is wrong of me to do so, no doubt, but I shall do so all the same."

A frown pulled at Oliver's forehead.

"If it is wrong, then I do not want to know of it, Lady Guilford."

She tutted.

"That is not to say that it is *wrong*, only that I am sure she would wish to tell you herself but, given the circumstances, she has not been able to do so."

"Circumstances?" Oliver blinked, his frown lifting. "I am unsure as to what you mean."

Lady Guilford threw up her hands.

"Are you not listening to me, Lord Edenbridge? This is of the greatest importance!"

Trying all the more to understand, Oliver gestured to a chair.

"Might you wish to sit down, Lady Guilford?"

"No." She took a deep breath, then lifted her chin. "I am sorry if I appear a little fraught, Lord Edenbridge. There is a good deal of weight in this and that is why I have now come to speak with you."

"I see." Not understanding in the least, Oliver put a smile on his lips and silently prayed that the lady might soon start speaking in terms that he could understand. "What is it that you wish to tell me, Lady Guilford?"

She took a breath, then let it out slowly, closing her eyes for a moment as though to calm herself.

"Lord Edenbridge, at your masquerade ball, I believe that you were in conversation with the lady who writes for The London Chronicle."

A sudden thrill ran up Oliver's spine.

"Yes, I was. Why, do you know of her?"

The lady smiled.

"I am acquainted with her, actually. That is why I have come to speak with you. I believe that the conversation you were having with her was brought to a rather swift end, leaving it unfinished."

Oliver nodded, a little surprised at how much Lady Guilford knew.

"Yes, that is so."

"Might I suggest that you continue that conversation with her?"

Oliver's shoulders dropped.

"I cannot, given that I do not know who she is, Lady Guilford. Unless it is that you wish to tell me?"

Lady Guilford opened her mouth, closed it again, and then frowned.

"I – I am not sure that it would be right for me to do so. Believe me, Lord Guilford, I came here in the hope of telling you everything, but now that I am standing with you, now that I am in your company, I begin to see that this must be something she does on her own."

"But you think that there is more that she might wish to say."

It took a moment, but Lady Guilford not only nodded but smiled.

"More that she wishes to say, but also more that *you* will wish to share with her, I am certain." This was greatly confusing and though Oliver appreciated the lady's visit, he still could not understand what it was that she meant. "You should write to her, as you have done before," Lady Guilford continued, waving one hand in his direction as though she expected him to go and fetch his quill at that very moment. "Insist on speaking with her and, if she does not soon appear, then you must inform me, and I will bring you to her."

Oliver blinked in surprise.

"You will?"

"I will. It is vitally important to me that you meet the lady," she said, with a firmness that made Oliver's eyebrows lift all the more. "It must soon happen. It must be soon, for I fear that she will lose all hope otherwise."

It took all of Oliver's strength not to ask what hope it was that this mysterious lady might lose, but realizing that he would not be given a simple answer, he merely nodded.

"You will do it, then?"

"Yes, I will."

"Might you do it now?" she asked, astonishing him. "I

will take it myself to The London Chronicle so that it might be delivered to her."

"I am grateful for your willingness, but I am expecting Lord Dunstable and his betrothed to call very soon," Oliver answered, seeing the frustration fill Lady Guilford's expression. "But I shall write this very afternoon, I promise you."

Lady Guilford took a step closer to him, her eyes sharp.

"You swear it to me?"

"I do." Oliver put one hand to his heart and then bowed. "You have my word."

This seemed to satisfy Lady Guilford and, with a nod, she swept from the room, leaving Oliver staring after her. Whatever it was that she knew, whoever this lady was, it was clear that Lady Guilford was quite determined that she and Oliver would soon meet. With a shake of his head, Oliver sat back down, feeling the urge to pull out a sheet of paper and begin his letter, only for a knock on the door to interrupt him.

"Come in." He beamed as Lord Dunstable walked into the room, reaching out to shake his hand quickly. "My friend. I am glad to see you." His smile faded just a little as the door closed behind Lord Dunstable without Lady Henrietta coming into the room. "Your betrothed?"

"All is well, have no fear," came the reply. "She was unable to call upon you with me, for she is preparing her trousseau." Perhaps seeing Oliver's surprise, Lord Dunstable shrugged. "Her father has been good enough to keep back Lady Henrietta's dowry, it seems. He has not gambled it away, as she feared, and thus, there is enough for her to spend on the trousseau before we wed." His shoulders fell. "I did tell them all that I had no need of her dowry, but her father was quite insistent. Mayhap he feels a little ashamed after all he has done, I do not know."

"Then I am very glad for you."

"You will come to the service, will you not?"

Oliver threw out his hands.

"Of course I will! Nothing could prevent me from joining you on your wedding day."

His friend tilted his head just a little, his gaze steadying.

"I am sorry that you are not to have such a day yourself. I know that you are glad for my sake, and for Lady Henrietta's, that we have found such a connection, but I did hear about Miss Leverton also."

Oliver looked away.

"It is unexpected, certainly, to be left without any young lady in my consideration. It is not what I expected!"

"And is there no other?"

A frown darted across Oliver's forehead.

"Another? Another lady I have been considering, you mean?"

Lord Dunstable nodded.

"No, there is not. You know that I was only seeking out Lady Henrietta and Miss Leverton. Who else could you be thinking of?"

"Lady Harsham."

Lord Dunstable did not hesitate, speaking quite plainly and making Oliver's heart leap in surprise.

"She does not... that is to say, she will not be considering any gentleman in such a light," Oliver answered, ignoring the way that his heart ached as he spoke. "I did not mean to overhear, but overhear I did, and she made it quite plain that she had no intention of ever marrying again."

Lord Dunstable's eyebrow lifted.

"Then might I ask, if she *was* willing to consider you in that light, would you then find yourself more amenable to the idea?"

Oliver swallowed, hard, aware of just how much that would mean to him, should he permit himself to think of it. Lady Harsham had often come to his heart and mind, particularly of late, and he had to admit to himself that their strong connection was one that he valued.

"I – I cannot say."

"Yes, you can. You simply do not wish to."

"Well, what is it that you want me to admit?" Oliver asked, suddenly agitated, throwing up his hands. "Should you like me to say that yes, I find Lady Harsham more delightful than any young lady of my acquaintance? That our connection is so strong, I cannot think of it weakening without great pain?" He began to walk about the room, gesticulating as he went, heat burning through him. "Would you like me to confess that, had I any hope of a return of my feelings, I would declare myself interested in furthering our connection? There is no hope, my friend, and thus, I have no thought of such things."

Lord Dunstable blinked furiously, and Oliver ran one hand down over his face, feeling a little embarrassed. He had said more than he intended, revealed more than he had realized was within his heart – and Lord Dunstable seemed to recognize that.

"You have an affection for her then, yes?" Lord Dunstable spoke quietly but his words were like thunder-claps, forcing Oliver to consider his own heart with a frank-ness he had not done before. "I have seen your connection to Lady Harsham grow these last few weeks and, truth be told, I did wonder if your interest in her might overshadow your pursuit of the other two ladies in question. I hoped that you would realize that your interest in Lady Harsham was more than just a friendship, before you even thought of asking one of the others to court – and indeed, I would have spoken to you about all of this, should you have told me of your intention to do so."

"I – it does not matter how I feel." Oliver's chest was tight and his voice a little strained. "She has already made it clear that there can be no connection between us, aside from friendship."

"But she did not say that directly to you."

Oliver shook his head.

"But she does not need to. I am glad that I know of it for then it meant that I would not make myself foolish in seeking out something which she could not, or did not want to offer."

"Yet that also means you have not been honest with yourself and your own heart," Lord Dunstable said, quietly. "And though you might have been a fool in speaking honestly, you might also have found something rather surprising in your connection to the lady. Mayhap, despite what you overheard her say, she might have her own feelings which she is battling with."

Closing his eyes, Oliver let out a slow breath.

"I cannot be sure of that."

"That is why you must take a risk. Though I will say, what I have seen of her when she is with you tells me that there might be something more there. Something that you, as yet, have not seen."

Oliver blinked, then frowned, wanting to refute his friend's words but, at the same time, surprised at just how much his heart leaped with the sudden hope that was offered him.

"Will you think about what I have said, at least?" Lord Dunstable asked as Oliver rubbed one hand over his eyes. "I should like to see you happy, and I am sure that Lady

Harsham would be the one to make you so – just as you might make her happy in return."

Nodding, Oliver cleared his throat rather gruffly, feeling a trifle uncomfortable at having spoken so honestly but also a little confused with all that he had revealed – even to himself.

"I will think about it, yes."

"Good." Lord Dunstable winked. "And mayhap there will be two weddings very soon, instead of just the one."

CHAPTER TWENTY

I must do this.

Jane was trembling all over as the butler directed her to Lord Edenbridge's drawing room. She had considered everything that Lady Guilford had said, had paced up and down the room, spent a fitful night tossing and turning, cried many tears and, in the end, found the resolve to do what she knew she must.

Though now that she was being shown into the drawing room, now that he was standing, rising to greet her with a warm smile on his handsome face, she felt her courage fail her.

"Jane." Lord Edenbridge reached out, took her hand, and much to Jane's surprise, brought it to his lips as he bowed over it. "How delighted I am to see you."

"You appear to be in good spirits," Jane answered, forcing a smile. "I am glad to see that. I know that you have been troubled with all that has just been revealed, and you have had much to consider."

"I have, but I have discovered a new happiness," he answered, gesturing for her to sit down, though he took a seat angled just beside her so that he might look into her eyes – a closeness which Jane found a little disconcerting, given all that she had to say. "I was going to come and call on you myself, in fact, though it seems that you have saved me the trouble!"

Jane swallowed thickly and tried to smile. The words were there for her to speak but they would not come and thus, silence filled the space between them for some minutes.

Then, Lord Edenbridge leaned a little closer and, putting his hand on top of hers, gazed back at her.

"You appear a little ill at ease, Jane. Are you quite all right?"

Nodding, Jane closed her eyes.

"I – I am well. It is only that there is something I wish to tell you."

"Oh?"

His hand had not left hers and heat began to prickle up Jane's arm, going straight to her heart, where a fluttering sensation had begun.

"I wanted to tell you that..." Closing her eyes to shut out the sight of him, Jane took in another steadying breath. "I wanted to tell you that I received your letter."

Silence was her only response and, opening her eyes, Jane looked into the face of Lord Edenbridge, seeing him frown. She could say nothing more, watching as he searched her face, praying that somehow, understanding would come before she had to make any further explanations.

Then, Lord Edenbridge's breath caught in a gasp, his eyes flared wide and he stared at her with shock rippling across his expression.

Jane dropped her head.

"It was you?" he breathed, his hand now tightening on

hers rather than pulling away. "You are the one who has been writing to me, the one who responded at The London Chronicle?"

She could do nothing other than glance at him and give him the smallest of nods.

Lord Edenbridge rose suddenly, standing back from her, staring at her as though he had never seen her before, and a great and terrible fear rose up in Jane's heart. He was going to be angry with her, upset and broken that she had kept such things from him, was he not? He might ask her to leave his house, might demand that she no longer be in his acquaintance, and all because she had not told him the truth.

"You wore peacock feathers in your mask," he murmured, as Jane closed her eyes tightly, her fingers weaving together as she fought back against her fears. "You came to tell me about Miss Leverton and then were you not eager to say more?"

Tears burned behind Jane's eyes.

"I wanted to tell you the truth of who I was," she said, her voice rasping. "But then Lord Tertford came, and I could not continue." Opening her eyes again, she blinked back against her tears again, trying to keep him in focus. "I am sorry that I did not tell you before, but I did not feel that it was necessary and, truth be told, I hesitated because I did not always want to admit to anyone else that I had employment. I know that you must be angry with me for hiding that part of myself from you–"

"Angry?" Lord Edenbridge interrupted her, sounding astonished as she nodded. "No, Jane, not in the least!" He hurried towards her now, bending down in front of her, covering her hands with his. "Jane, I am overjoyed!"

The fear that had held her shattered in an instant, her

breath hitching as she tried to understand, astonished at the smile which was spreading wide across his face.

"You – you are?"

"Of course I am! I have wondered who this wise, kind creature might be, only to realize that the wise, kind lady that I already know, that I already call a dear friend, is the very same! I should have guessed, mayhap, that you were the writer at The London Chronicle, and your consideration of me and your gentle encouragements have been the only things to bolster my heart."

A dear friend. There was a slight tinge of sadness now in Jane's faint smile, realizing that though he was glad to know the truth, though he was happy to hear that she was the one that had been writing to, there was nothing more to their connection for him than that.

"I am relieved that you have accepted the truth so easily," she told him, squeezing his fingers back gently. "Thank you for your understanding."

"Thank you for all that you did for me."

Jane let out a slightly broken laugh, looking away from him.

"Though I am sorry that it did not bring you success."

There came a momentary pause, only for Lord Edenbridge to lean a fraction closer, forcing her gaze back to him simply by his nearness.

"Oh, but I think that it did." Jane did not know what he meant. The look in his eyes made her feel as though she had stepped out of a cold rain into a warm room where the fire burned hot in the grate. When a slow, small smile began to cross his lips, Jane shivered, though it was not from fear, but rather from a tiny flare of hope which began to burn in her heart. "You have made me feel a good many things of late, Jane." Lord Edenbridge, perhaps seeing that she was not about to speak aloud, rose to his feet, only to then come and sit directly beside her. "But the truth is, I have kept all of those emotions back from myself because I know that you have no interest in pursuing any sort of closer connection with me."

Her breath hitched, her eyes widening.

"I do not... how do you know such a thing?"

"Because I confess that I overheard you speaking to your friend as regards your late husband," he told her, making Jane's eyes squeeze closed. "I have never pressed you to tell me of all that you suffered, and I never would, but from what I heard, it seems to me as though he was not a kind gentleman."

Jane swallowed hard, tears beginning to threaten all over again.

"He was the most cruel man," she answered, looking back at him again. "I cannot tell you of the extent of it all. But society did not know him as that, my own father, I am sure, did not know of all that he was... of all that he could be."

"And you are afraid that, should you trust another gentleman, you might well find yourself caught in the same situation?"

With a small sigh, Jane's shoulders rounded as she nodded.

"Yes. I think that is so."

Her eyes caught his, watching him as he took in a breath, his dark brown eyes searching, filled with questions that she did not know how to answer.

Then, he spoke.

"Even with me?"

Jane's heart tumbled over in her chest, her breathing coming in quick gasps as she saw, for the first time, the hope that flared in his expression and which she too felt in her heart. She did not know what to say, could find no words to express the rushing emotions she felt... and yet, the answer was there.

"Perhaps I should not have asked you." Lord Edenbridge closed his eyes and then dropped his head, giving it a small shake. "Forgive me, I–"

"I have been afraid." He lifted his head. "I have been afraid of what you might be hiding," she continued, her words beginning to tumble now, one over the other as she finally found the strength to speak. "I have wrestled with it, telling myself that I am contented to let you pursue others and ignoring the wound that your interest in Lady Henrietta and Miss Leverton created." Her voice was shaking but she grasped his hand, desperate now for him to see, to understand. "Louisa told me that you were not like my husband was and, as I have considered it, the more I have realized that my fear is what has taken me captive, and held me back from telling you the truth of my feelings."

Lord Edenbridge's fingers tightened around hers.

"I can understand your fear, Jane." He leaned a fraction closer. "It may only be words, but I want to assure you that I am just as you see me. There may be times when I grow frustrated and upset – as I believe you have already seen when we first met, in fact – but I have never caused injury to another because of it. My words can be sharp at times, but they would never knowingly cause injury, especially not to someone I loved."

Jane gasped and Lord Edenbridge did the same, leaving them both staring at each other, wide-eyed. She could not quite believe what she had heard and, evidently, Lord Edenbridge could not quite believe what he had said. Dare she trust that his words were true? Dare she believe that he spoke the truth of his heart?

"Goodness." Lord Edenbridge began to chuckle, and Jane's lips curved upwards, her heart burning with hope, with excitement, and with love. "I had not put words to what I felt, for it has been a fairly new consideration, but it seems now, Jane, that my heart has betrayed me to you." Lifting his hand, he touched her cheek, then settled it to her shoulder. "I think all that I feel means that I am in love with you, my dear."

Jane's eyes filled with tears, though she smiled through them, her heart overflowing now with all that she felt. It was as though, hearing him speak those words, she had finally permitted herself to admit all that she felt.

"Then, Edenbridge, I must also confess that I believe I am in love with you. I have never felt such a strength, such a depth of feeling before, but the truth is, I cannot imagine being separated from you. I know that if you had begun to court another, my heart would have been torn with a pain far greater than anything I have ever felt before."

"Then I am glad that they both stepped away from me and into the arms of others," he answered, leaning a little closer still. "For it meant that I could see exactly who it was my heart longed for." His fingers brushed her neck and Jane shivered in delight. "I will not push you into any sort of commitment, Jane. I want you to be able to trust me fully, to know me as well as you know yourself."

"I do trust you," she said, quickly, "it was the fear from my past lurching forward, attempting to take hold of the happiness I now feel, stealing it away from me." Pressing her lips together for a moment, she took a deep breath and then smiled. "Will you court me, Edenbridge?"

Lord Edenbridge's expression lit with surprise, only for him to laugh gently as he moved closer, lowering his head.

"I should be delighted to, Jane."

She realized that he was not about to close the distance between them and kiss her, as it was clear that he wanted to do. The respect he showed her, the understanding in his actions, and his patience made her heart burn with love for him all the more. With a momentary pause to catch her breath, Jane leaned forward and settled her lips to his. After a moment of shocked stillness, he relaxed, his lips moving softly against hers.

It was the first time she had kissed someone who loved her, the first time she had felt safe and secure in an embrace. Melting into his arms, Jane let her arms wrap around his neck as he held her tight, trusting that he would never let her go.

I AM so glad Jane was able to overcome her fear of men and found love!

Did you miss the first book in the Whispers of the Ton series? Check out The Truth about the Earl in the Kindle Store. Read ahead for a sneak peek!

MY DEAR READER

Thank you for reading and supporting my books! I hope this story brought you some escape from the real world into the always captivating Regency world. A good story, especially one with a happy ending, just brightens your day and makes you feel good! If you enjoyed the book, would you leave a review on Amazon? Reviews are always appreciated.

Below is a complete list of all my books! Why not click and see if one of them can keep you entertained for a few hours?

The Duke's Daughters Series
The Duke's Daughters: A Sweet Regency Romance Boxset
A Rogue for a Lady
My Restless Earl
Rescued by an Earl
In the Arms of an Earl
The Reluctant Marquess (Prequel)

A Smithfield Market Regency Romance
The Smithfield Market Romances: A Sweet Regency
Romance Boxset
The Rogue's Flower
Saved by the Scoundrel
Mending the Duke
The Baron's Malady

The Returned Lords of Grosvenor Square
The Returned Lords of Grosvenor Square: A Regency
Romance Boxset
The Waiting Bride
The Long Return
The Duke's Saving Grace
A New Home for the Duke

The Spinsters Guild
The Spinsters Guild: A Sweet Regency Romance Boxset
A New Beginning
The Disgraced Bride
A Gentleman's Revenge
A Foolish Wager
A Lord Undone

Convenient Arrangements
Convenient Arrangements: A Regency Romance
Collection
A Broken Betrothal
In Search of Love
Wed in Disgrace
Betrayal and Lies
A Past to Forget
Engaged to a Friend

Landon House
Landon House: A Regency Romance Boxset
Mistaken for a Rake
A Selfish Heart
A Love Unbroken
A Christmas Match
A Most Suitable Bride

An Expectation of Love

Second Chance Regency Romance
Second Chance Regency Romance Boxset
Loving the Scarred Soldier
Second Chance for Love
A Family of her Own
A Spinster No More

Soldiers and Sweethearts
Soldiers and Sweethearts Boxset
To Trust a Viscount
Whispers of the Heart
Dare to Love a Marquess
Healing the Earl
A Lady's Brave Heart

Ladies on their Own: Governesses and Companions
Ladies on their Own Boxset
More Than a Companion
The Hidden Governess
The Companion and the Earl
More than a Governess
Protected by the Companion

Lost Fortunes, Found Love
Lost Fortunes, Found Love Boxset
A Viscount's Stolen Fortune
For Richer, For Poorer
Her Heart's Choice
A Dreadful Secret
Their Forgotten Love
His Convenient Match

Only for Love
Only for Love : A Clean Regency Boxset
The Heart of a Gentleman
A Lord or a Liar
The Earl's Unspoken Love
The Viscount's Unlikely Ally
The Highwayman's Hidden Heart
Miss Millington's Unexpected Suitor

Waltzing with Wallflowers
The Wallflower's Unseen Charm
The Wallflower's Midnight Waltz
Wallflower Whispers
The Ungainly Wallflower
The Determined Wallflower
The Wallflower's Secret (Revenge of the Wallflowers series)
The Wallflower's Choice

Whispers of the Ton
The Truth about the Earl
The Truth about the Rogue
The Truth about the Marquess

Christmas in London Series
The Uncatchable Earl
The Undesirable Duke

Christmas Kisses Series
Christmas Kisses Box Set
The Lady's Christmas Kiss
The Viscount's Christmas Queen
Her Christmas Duke

Christmas Stories
Love and Christmas Wishes: Three Regency Romance
Novellas
A Family for Christmas
Mistletoe Magic: A Regency Romance
Heart, Homes & Holidays: A Sweet Romance Anthology

Happy Reading!
   All my love,
   Rose

A SNEAK PEEK OF THE
TRUTH ABOUT THE EARL

"$\mathcal{I}$ was very sorry to hear of the death of your husband."

Lady Norah Essington gave the older lady a small smile, which she did not truly feel. "I thank you. You are very kind." Her tone was dull but Norah had no particular concerns as regarded either how she sounded or how she appeared to the lady. She was, yet again, alone in the world, and as things stood, was uncertain as to what her future would be.

"You did not care for him, I think."

Norah's gaze returned to Lady Gillingham's with such force, the lady blinked in surprise and leaned back a fraction in her chair.

"I mean no harm by such words, I assure you. I –"

"You have made an assumption, Lady Gillingham, and I would be glad if you should keep such notions to yourself." Norah lifted her chin but heard her voice wobble. "I should prefer to mourn the loss of my husband without whispers or gossip chasing around after me."

Lady Gillingham smiled, reached forward, and settled one hand over Norah's. "But of course."

Norah turned her head, trying to silently signal that the meeting was now at an end. She was not particularly well acquainted with the lady and, as such, would be glad of her departure so that she might sit alone and in peace. Besides which, if Lady Gillingham had been as bold as to make such a claim as that directly to Norah herself, then what would she think to say to the *ton*? Society might be suddenly full of whispers about Norah and her late husband—and then what would she do?

"I have upset you. Forgive me."

Norah dared a glance at Lady Gillingham, taking in the gentle way her eyes searched Norah's face and the small, soft smile on her lips. "I do not wish you to disparage my late husband, Lady Gillingham. Nor do I want to hear such rumors being spread in London – whenever it would be that I would have cause to return."

"I quite understand, and I can assure you I do not have any intention of speaking of any such thing to anyone in society."

"Then why state such a thing in my presence? My husband is only a sennight gone and, as I am sure you are aware, I am making plans to remove myself to his estate."

"Provided you are still welcome there."

Norah closed her eyes, a familiar pain flashing through her heart. "Indeed." Suddenly, she wanted very much for Lady Gillingham to take her leave. This was not at all what she had thought would occur. The lady, she had assumed, would simply express her sympathies and take her leave.

"Again, I have injured you." Lady Gillingham let out a long sigh and then shook her head. "Lady Essington, forgive me. I am speaking out of turn and with great thoughtlessness, which I must apologize for. The truth is, I come here out of genuine concern for you, given that I have been in the very same situation."

Norah drew her eyebrows together. She was aware that Lady Gillingham was widowed but did not know when such a thing had taken place.

"I was, at that time, given an opportunity which I grasped at with both hands. It is a paid position but done most discreetly."

Blinking rapidly, Norah tried to understand what Lady Gillingham meant. "I am to be offered employment?" She shook her head. "Lady Gillingham, that is most kind of you but I assure you I will be quite well. My husband often assured me his brother is a kind, warm-hearted gentleman and I have every confidence that he will take care of me." This was said with a confidence Norah did not truly feel but given the strangeness of this first meeting, she was doing so in an attempt to encourage Lady Gillingham to take her leave. Her late husband had, in fact, warned her about his brother on more than one occasion, telling her he was a selfish, arrogant sort who would not care a jot for anyone other than himself.

"I am very glad to hear of it, but should you find yourself in any difficulty, then I would beg of you to consider this. I have written for the paper for some time and find myself a little less able to do so nowadays. The truth is, Lady Essington, I am a little dull when it comes to society and very little takes place that could be of any real interest to anyone, I am sure."

Growing a little frustrated, Norah spread her hands. "I do not understand you, Lady Gillingham. Perhaps this is not -"

"An opportunity to *write*, Lady Essington." Lady

Gillingham leaned forward in her chair, her eyes suddenly dark and yet sparkling at the same time. "To write about society! Do you understand what I mean?"

Norah shook her head but a small twist of interest flickered in her heart. "No, Lady Gillingham. I am afraid I do not."

The lady smiled and her eyes held fast to Norah's. "*The London Chronicle*, as you know, has society pages. I am sure you have read them?"

Norah nodded slowly, recalling the times she and her mother had pored over the society pages in search of news as to which gentlemen might be worth considering when it came to her future. "I have found them very informative."

"Indeed, I am glad to hear so." Lady Gillingham smiled as if she had something to do with the pages themselves. "There is a rather large column within the society pages that mayhap you have avoided if you are averse to gossip and the like."

Norah shifted uncomfortably in her chair. The truth was, she *had* read them many times over and had been a little too eager to know of the gossip and rumors swirling through London society whilst, at the same time, refusing to speak of them to anyone else for fear of spreading further gossip.

"I can see you understand what it is I am speaking about. Well, Lady Essington, you must realize that someone writes such a column, I suppose?" She smiled and Norah nodded slowly. "*I* am that person."

Shock spread through Norah's heart and ice filled her chest. Not all of the gossip she had read had been pleasant – indeed, some of it had been so very unfavorable that reputations had been quite ruined.

"You are a little surprised but I must inform you I have

set a great deal of trust in you by revealing this truth." Lady Gillingham's smile had quite faded and instead, Norah was left with a tight-lipped older lady looking back at her with steel in her dark eyes.

"I – I understand."

"Good." Lady Gillingham smiled but there was no lightness in her expression. "The reason I speak to you so, Lady Essington, is to offer you the opportunity in the very same way that I was all those years ago."

For some moments, Norah stared at Lady Gillingham with undisguised confusion. She had no notion as to what the lady meant nor what she wanted and, as such, could only shake her head.

Lady Gillingham sighed. "I am tired of writing my column, Lady Essington. As I have said, it is a paid position and all done very discreetly. I wish to return to my little house in the country and enjoy being away in the quiet countryside rather than the hubbub of London. The funds I have received for writing this particular column have been more than enough over the years and I have managed to save a good deal so that I might retire to the country in comfort."

"I see." Still a little confused, Norah twisted her lips to one side for a few moments. "And you wish for *me* to write this for you?"

"For yourself!" Lady Gillingham flung her hands in the air. "They want to continue the column, for it is *very* popular, and as such, they require someone to write it. I thought that, since you find yourself in much the same situation as I was some years ago, you might be willing to think on it."

Blowing out a long, slow breath, Norah found herself nodding out but quickly stopped it from occurring. "I think I should like to consider it a little longer."

"But of course. You have your mourning period, and thereafter, perhaps you might be willing to give me an answer?"

Norah frowned. "But that is a little over a year away."

"Yes, I am well aware it is a long time, Lady Essington. But I shall finish writing for this Season in the hope that you will take over thereafter. It is, as I am sure you have been able to tell, quite secretive and without any danger."

Norah gave her a small smile, finding her heart flooding with a little relief. "Because you are Mrs. Fullerton," she answered, as Lady Gillingham beamed at her. "You write as Mrs. Fullerton, I should say."

"Indeed, I do. I must, for else society would not wish to have me join them in anything, and then where would I be?" A murmur of laughter broke from her lips as she got to her feet, bringing her prolonged visit to an end. "Consider what I have suggested, my dear. I do not know what your circumstances are at present and I am quite certain you will *not* be aware of them until you return to the late Lord Essington's estate but I am quite sure you would do excellently. You may, of course, write to me whenever you wish with any questions or concerns that I could answer for you."

"I very much appreciate your concern *and* your consideration, Lady Gillingham." Rising to her feet, Norah gave the lady a small curtsy, which was returned. "I shall take the year to consider it."

"Do." Reaching out, Lady Gillingham grasped Norah's hands and held them tightly, her eyes fixed on Norah's. "Do not permit yourself to be pushed aside, Lady Essington. Certain characters might soon determine that you do not deserve what is written on Lord Essington's will but be aware that it cannot be contested. Take what is yours and make certain you do all you can for your comfort. No one will take from you what is rightfully yours, I assure you."

Norah's smile slipped and she could only nod as Lady Gillingham squeezed her hands. She was rather fearful of returning to her late husband's estate and being informed of her situation as regarded her husband's death.

"And you must promise me that you will not speak of this to anyone."

"Of course," Norah promised without hesitation. "I shall not tell a soul, Lady Gillingham. Of that, you can be quite certain."

"Good, I am glad." With another warm smile, Lady Gillingham dropped Norah's hands and made her way to the door. "Good afternoon, Miss Essington. I do hope your sorrow passes quickly."

Norah nodded and smiled but did not respond. Did Lady Gillingham know Norah had never had a kind thought for her husband? That their marriage had been solely because of Lord Essington's desire to have a young, pretty wife by his side rather than due to any real or genuine care or consideration for her? Telling herself silently that such a thing did not matter, Norah waited until Lady Gillingham had quit the room before flopping back into her chair and blowing out a long breath.

Most extraordinary. Biting her lip, Norah considered what Lady Gillingham had offered her. Was it something she would consider? Would she become the next writer of the *London Chronicle* society column? It was employment, but not something Norah could simply ignore.

"I might very well require some extra coin," she murmured to herself, sighing heavily as another rap came at the door. Most likely, this would be another visitor coming to express their sympathy and sorrow. Whilst Norah did not begrudge them, she was finding herself rather weary.

I have a year to consider, she reminded herself, calling for the footman to come into the room. *One year. And then I may very well find myself as the new Mrs. Fullerton.*

CHAPTER ONE

*O*ne *year later.*
    Taking the hand of her coachman, Norah descended from the carriage and drew in a long breath.
I am back in London.

The strange awareness that she was quite alone – without companion or chaperone – rushed over her, rendering Norah a little uncomfortable. Wriggling her shoulders a little in an attempt to remove such feelings from herself, Norah put a smile on her face and began to walk through St James' Park, praying that Lady Gillingham would be waiting as she had promised.

The last year had been something of a dull one and it brought Norah a good deal of pleasure to be back in town. Society had been severely lacking and the only other people in the world she had enjoyed conversation with had been her lady's maid, Cherry, and the housekeeper. Both had seemed to recognize that Norah was a little lonely and as the months had passed, a semblance of friendship – albeit a strange one – had begun to flourish. However, upon her return to town, Norah had been forced to leave both the maid and the housekeeper behind, for she was no longer permitted to reside in the small estate that had been hers for the last year. Now, she was to find a way to settle in London and with an entirely new complement of staff.

"Ah, Lady Essington! I am so glad to see you again."

Lady Gillingham rose quickly from where she had been seated on the small, wooden bench and, much to Norah's surprise, grasped her hands tightly whilst looking keenly into her eyes.

"I do hope you are well?"

Norah nodded, a prickling running down her spine. "I am quite well, I thank you."

"You have been looked after this past year?"

Opening her mouth to say that yes, she was quite satisfied, Norah slowly closed it again and saw the flicker of understanding in Lady Gillingham's eye.

"The newly titled Lord Essington did not wish for me to reside with him so I was sent to the dower house for the last few months," she explained, as Lady Gillingham's jaw tightened. "I believe that Lord Essington has spent the time attempting to find a way to remove from me what my late husband bequeathed but he has been unable to do so."

Lady Gillingham's eyes flared and a small smile touched the corner of her mouth. "I am very glad to hear it."

"I have a residence here in London and a small complement of staff." It was not quite the standard she was used to but Norah was determined to make the best of it. "I do not think I shall be able to purchase any new gowns - although it may be required of me somehow – but I am back in town, at the very least."

Lady Gillingham nodded, turned, and began to walk along the path, gesturing for Norah to fall into step with her. "You were given only a small yearly allowance?"

Norah shrugged one shoulder lightly. "It is more than enough to take care of my needs, certainly."

"But not enough to give you any real ease."

Tilting her head, Norah considered what she said, then chose to push away her pride and nod.

"It is as you say." There would be no additional expenses, no new gowns, gloves, or bonnets and she certainly could not eat extravagantly but at least she had a comfortable home. "The will stated that I was to have the furnished townhouse in London and that my brother-in-law is liable for all repairs to keep it to a specific standard for the rest of my remaining life and that, certainly, is a comfort."

"I can see that it is, although might you consider marrying again?"

Norah hesitated. "It is not something I have given a good deal of thought to, Lady Gillingham. I have had a great deal of loss these last few years, with the passing of my mother shortly after my marriage and, thereafter, the passing of Lord Essington himself. To find myself now back in London without a parent or husband is a little strange, and I confess that I find it a trifle odd. However, for the moment, it is a freedom that I wish to explore rather than remove from myself in place of another marriage."

Lady Gillingham laughed and the air around them seemed to brighten. "I quite understand. I, of course, never married again and there is not always a desire to do so, regardless. That is quite an understandable way of thinking and you must allow yourself time to become accustomed to your new situation."

"Yes, I think you are right."

Tilting her head slightly, Lady Gillingham looked side-long at Norah. "And have you given any consideration to my proposal?"

Norah hesitated, her stomach dropping. Until this moment, she had been quite determined that she would *not* do as Lady Gillingham had asked, whereas now she was no longer as certain. Realizing she would have to live a somewhat frugal life for the rest of her days *or* marry a gentleman with a good deal more fortune – which was, of course, somewhat unlikely since she was a widow – the idea of earning a little more coin was an attractive one.

"I – I was about to refuse until this moment. But now that I am back in your company, I feel quite changed."

Lady Gillingham's eyes lit up. "Truthfully?"

Letting out a slightly awkward laugh, Norah nodded. "Although I am not certain I shall have the same way with words as you. How do you find such interesting stories?"

The burst of laughter that came from Lady Gillingham astonished Norah to the point that her steps slowed significantly.

"Oh, forgive me, Lady Essington! It is clear you have not plunged the depths of society as I have."

A slow flush of heat crept up Norah's cheeks. "It is true that I was very well protected from any belligerent gentlemen and the like. My mother was most fastidious."

"As she ought." Lady Gillingham attempted to hide her smile but it fought to remain on her lips. "But you shall find society a very different beast now, Lady Essington!"

Norah shivered, not certain that she liked that particular remark.

"You are a widowed lady, free to do as you please and act as you wish. You will find that both the gentlemen and ladies of the *ton* will treat you very differently now and that, Lady Essington, is where you will find all manner of stories being brought to your ears."

"I see."

A small frown pulled at Lady Gillingham's brow. "However, I made certain any stories I wrote had a basis in fact. I do not like to spread rumors unnecessarily. I stayed far from stories that would bring grave injury to certain parties."

Norah nodded slowly, seeing the frown and realizing just how seriously Lady Gillingham had taken her employment.

"There is a severe responsibility that must be considered before you take this on, Lady Essington. You must be aware that whatever you write *will* have consequences."

Pressing her lips together tightly, Norah thought about this for a few moments. "I recall that my mother and I used to read the society papers very carefully indeed, to make certain we would not keep company with any gentlemen who were considered poorly by the *ton*."

Lady Gillingham nodded. "Indeed, that is precisely what I mean. If a lady had been taken advantage of, then I would never write about her for fear of what that might entail. However, I would make mention of the gentleman in question, in some vague, yet disparaging, way that made certain to keep the rest of the debutantes away from him."

"I understand."

"We may not be well acquainted, Lady Essington, but I have been told of your kind and sweet nature by others. I believe they thought very well of your mother and, in turn, of you."

Norah put her hand to her heart, an ache in her throat. "I thank you."

Lady Gillingham smiled softly. "So what say you, Lady Essington? Will you do as I have long hoped?"

"Will I write under the name of Mrs. Fullerton?" A slow, soft smile pulled at her lips as she saw Lady

Gillingham nod. "And when would they wish their first piece?"

Lady Gillingham shrugged. "I write every week about what I have discovered. Sometimes the article is rather long and sometimes it is very short. The amount you write does not matter. It is what it contains that is of interest. They will pay you the same amount, regardless."

"They?" Norah pricked up her ears at the mention of money. "And might I ask how much is being offered?"

Norah's eyes widened as Lady Gillingham told her of the very large amount that would be given to her for every piece written. *That would allow me to purchase one new gown at the very least!*

"And it is the man in charge of the *London Chronicle* that has asked me for this weekly contribution. In time, you will be introduced to him. But that is only if you are willing to take on the role?"

Taking in a deep breath, Norah let it out slowly and closed her eyes for a moment. "Yes, I think I shall."

Lady Gillingham clapped her hands together in delight, startling a nearby blackbird. "How wonderful! I shall, of course, be glad to assist you with your first article. Thereafter, I fully intend to return to my house in the countryside and remain far away from *all* that London society has to offer." Her smile faded as she spoke, sending a stab of worry into Norah's heart. Could it be that after years of writing such articles, of being in amongst society and seeing all that went on, Lady Gillingham was weary of the *ton*? Norah swallowed hard and tried to push her doubts away. This was to bring her a little more coin and, therefore, a little more ease. After all that she had endured these last few years, that would be of the greatest comfort to her.

"So, when are you next to go into society?"

Norah looked at Lady Gillingham. "I have only just come to London. I believe I have an invitation to Lord Henderson's ball tomorrow evening, however."

"As have I." Lady Gillingham looped her arm through Norah's, as though they were suddenly great friends. "We shall attend together and I will help you find not only what you are to write about but I shall also introduce you to various gentlemn and ladies that you might wish to befriend."

A little confused, Norah frowned. "For what purpose?"

"Oh, some gentlemen, in particular, will have *excellent* potential when it comes to your writings. You do not have to like them – indeed, it is best if you do *not*, for your conscience's sake."

Norah's spirits dropped low. Was this truly the right thing for her to be doing? She did not want to injure gentlemen and ladies unnecessarily, nor did she want to have guilt on her conscience. *But the money would be so very helpful.*

"I can choose what I write, yes?"

Lady Gillingham glanced over at her sharply. "Yes, of course."

"And the newspaper will not require me to write any falsehoods?"

Lady Gillingham shook her head. "No, indeed not."

Norah set her shoulders. "Then I shall do as you have done and write what I think is only best for society to know, in order to protect debutantes and the like from any uncouth gentlemen."

"That is fair." Lady Gillingham smiled and Norah took in a long breath, allowing herself to smile as she settled the matter with her conscience. "I am sure you shall do very well indeed, Lady Essington."

Norah tilted her head up toward the sky for a moment as a sense of freedom burst over her once again. "I must hope so, Lady Gillingham. The ball will be a very interesting evening indeed, I am sure."

I THINK the society column will yield some very interesting stories, don't you? I hope Lady Essington does well! Check out the rest of the story in the Kindle Store The Truth about the Earl

JOIN MY MAILING LIST AND FACEBOOK READER GROUP

Sign up for my newsletter to stay up to date on new releases, contests, giveaways, freebies, and deals!

Free book with signup!

Monthly Facebook Giveaways! Books and Amazon gift cards!
Join my reader group on Facebook!

Rose's Ravenous Readers

Facebook Page: https://www. facebook.com/rosepearsonauthor

Website: www.RosePearsonAuthor.com
You can sign up for my Newsletter on my website too!

Follow me on Goodreads: Author Page